THE FINAL SOLUTION

THE
FINAL
SOLUTION

by

STEPHEN
WEINSTEIN

American BookWorks Corporation
Ridgefield, CT

The text of this book is composed in Garamond with display type set in Goudy Handtooled.

Designed by MARTIN DUFOUR

Cover design by ULLA KLING ATKINSON

ISBN 0-9622813-2-8
10 9 8 7 6 5 4 3 2 1

Printed in Canada.

To my wife Eva for improving my life.
To my son Alexander for improving my writing.

My gratitude and thanks to Avi and Dora Morrow.

"Art is a lie which makes us realize the truth."
— Picasso

Fiction serves a similar end.

CHAPTER ONE

Only a few hours left until the end of the world and Ari knew he was responsible for ending it.

It was of course an exaggeration. The world would not end. The globe upon which he stood would keep spinning, other than for a few momentary shrugs and the ensuing clouds of dust and heat. Most people would wake up and learn of what had happened from their radios or televisions. Others would read about it in their morning papers over a cup of coffee. But in one small part of the world, a part that had suffered from religious wars since recorded history, the part where Ari Ben Lev's wife and child lived, the conflict would finally come to an end. The Jewish State, and several million Arabs in reprisal, would cease to exist.

He'd set Armageddon's clock in motion. No matter that he willed it otherwise, he couldn't stop it now, no one could. He'd been shouting for hours for someone to listen. His voice, raw and strained, could now barely rise above a whisper.

Ari Ben Lev sat on the bed in his cell. He took no notice of the hard wire springs that pressed into him through the thin mattress. His thoughts were of David, his eight-year-old son, who was unlikely to celebrate another birthday. Ari buried his face in his hands. He wept, unconcerned by the eyes that watched him from behind the mirrored slit in the door of his cell. What did it matter who saw him? Death nullified such vanities.

It was to have been his triumph, his legacy. The discovery of a lifetime! A new source of energy, non polluting and virtually inexhaustible. It was supposed to change the world, not end it!

David's small body would be consumed along with the millions of others he'd unwittingly condemned. His son would never know a grave. There would be nothing but dust and no one left to mourn him.

Horrific images flashed in Ari's mind, transforming the ancient streets and buildings of Jerusalem, the golden city that for millennia people had fought and died for, into mounds of ash and rubble. It was like looking into the sun. Nothing would be left.

In another part of the same fortress-like building, a similar scene was playing itself out. The young soldier stationed outside Sidney Taylor's cell continued to monitor her every movement. He watched her pace the limits of the stone walls that confined her. She was a beautiful caged animal.

Like Ari, she knew that she was being observed. That no one responded to her entreaties felt like a violation, as did the unseen eyes beyond her cell, which invaded her solitude. As a scientist she was used to the microscope. Never before, however, had she been the object of study. She approached the door.

The guard knew it was impossible for the woman to see him through the one-way glass, but still he pulled away. He'd been watching her for hours, listening to her pleas. To see her face, this American beauty, with her golden hair tied back like a schoolgirl's, to look into those inviting soft green eyes, it was impossible for him to imagine she could be a danger to the State of Israel.

He wanted to reply, but knew he couldn't. He was under strict orders: *There was to be absolutely no contact. Contact between guard and the guarded could lead to empathy, which could in turn compromise one's effectiveness.* It was a critical part of his training, drilled into him by Eritz, a special branch of the Masad, Israel's secret service.

But what of the things she had said, the terrible warnings? He would relay them to his superior, once he was relieved of his post. Until then, orders were orders. It was not his job to decide. Others made those evaluations. Until he was told otherwise, she would continue to be held in total isolation.

"Why won't you answer me?" she pleaded. "For the love of God, listen to me!" She yelled, invoking the name of a God she no longer believed in. The existence of the all-loving God she'd grown up with in her parents' house no longer fit the world she knew.

There was no answer. The man outside her cell was as ethereal as her parents' God.

They had no right to treat her like this. She'd done nothing wrong; committed no crime. She was an American! Indignation bubbled up, momentarily overshadowing her fear. She had come to Israel to help, to stop the unimaginable. They refused to listen.

She fought not to cry. She wouldn't give them the satisfaction.

"Please," she pleaded for the final time.

Only silence met her appeal.

"Damn you all!" Her hand struck the door. The impact was negligible, the pain immediate. Her façade cracked. Tears filled her eyes. They spilled over, staining her cheeks. She struggled to get the words out:

"We're all going to die!" Her forehead pressed against the cold steel of the door.

As a scientist Sidney Taylor accepted the inevitability of death. As a woman in her early thirties, who was in love and wanted children, she was unwilling to accept that it could be her own.

Outside Israel there were others who knew what was to come. Some, like Ari and Sidney, would give anything to stop it. Others would do everything to make certain it wasn't stopped.

In Russia, General Alexander Primikov had made possible the transfer of technology. The decision hadn't been difficult. As a military man he was used to making such choices. The funds he received for the device were vital to finance his ascendancy to the presidency. It was merely a matter of expediency. Pieces moving on a chessboard, acceptable losses.

He was an ex-communist turned democrat, ex-general turned Minister of Energy. A man whose concern was neither for Muslim nor Jew, only for Russia. He'd watched his country taken apart, its greatness dismembered. He'd fought in Afghanistan, seen his men needlessly sacrificed by politicians in Moscow who lacked the stomach and commitment to do what needed to be done. He could have won, or so he believed, had they just given him the resources he'd requested. They had refused, while the Americans continued to supply and train the Mujahedin. The outcome was inevitable. He and his men had returned from the war in disgrace.

He would make those responsible pay for Russia's shame. The day of reckoning was coming. The disruptions in the Middle East would assure the importance of Russian oil. With the rocketing price of each gallon his personal power would grow exponentially.

A religious war was building. It was coming out of the east to threaten the balance of power of the world. Islamic fundamentalism had already stripped the USSR of its eastern republics.

What remained of Russia needed to be preserved by a strong president willing to sacrifice, whatever necessary, for its survival. It was his destiny to restore Russia to greatness.

In a remote area of Lebanon's Bekaa Valley, safely away from the center of the blast, Jabal Hussein, Minister of Defense of the Sword of God, moved through the command compound with a sense of invulnerability. He eagerly anticipated the attack he'd set in motion. He and his faithful, soldiers called terrorists by the West, were willing to die for the cause.

Call him what they liked! He had no use for the good graces of his enemies, descendants of the Saxon hordes who'd streamed across the water to plunder and murder under the name of a false God

It had taken generations to drive those early invaders back across the sea. His forefathers had reclaimed the land, only to have it stolen again. It would be reclaimed and this time he would be there to see it happen.

It was a pity, he thought, that Abud Rachman wouldn't share in the victory, but the Sword of God's founder had grown old and soft. The two had been close friends. Now they differed openly and their differences were splitting the organization apart. Rachman had changed from warrior to elder statesman, turning his back on everything the two had fought for and believed in. Rachman was willing to lay down the sword for empty promises on paper, to accept a small sliver of land, stolen from their people, in exchange for 'peace.' Jabal couldn't let that happen.

Only the sword could be trusted. There was a time when Rachman understood that as well as he did. Now, Rachman had become an obstacle, preventing those who would use the sword from striking at the enemy. He'd moved from an asset to a liability, unwilling to make the necessary decisions required of a military leader. Brutality was a weapon, fear a resource. Every time Jabal attempted to use them, Rachman was there to stop him.

There would be no compromise this time. If all went as planned it would be the name of Jabal Hussein, not Rachman, who would rise above the cleansing firestorm. It would be Jabal Hussein who would end the Zionist domination of their lands. He, not Abud Rachman, would avenge the deaths of their fathers and their martyred children. He, alone, would sound the trumpet of Jihad and raise the banner under which the faithful would follow.

The holy fire would burn itself clean. The land would be scorched, but in time the desert would bloom again. It was a huge price to pay, but that was the price of salvation. His people were in place, the hour had been set, the minutes were counting down. All that was left to do was to be patient, a quality that didn't come easily to him.

* * *

High above the daily hustle of New York City, Roger Glass, Chairman of RG Industries, the largest, privately held energy resource company in the world, stood in front of the floor-to-ceiling windows of his private office. He stared down at the water far below, watching the ships sail down the Hudson. The monitor in the wall unit behind him flashed out ever-changing images of international news. The sound on the set had been turned low, but when the announcement came he wouldn't miss it.

It had been his plan, his money and his connections. The loss of life was regrettable, but what he'd done he'd done for the greater good. In Israel's hands the technology would have plunged the world into economic chaos. It had to be stopped.

Still, the decision had not been easy. A lot of people were going to die, Sidney Taylor among them. She'd betrayed him, but her death brought him no pleasure. He recalled the small concentric lines that formed at the corners of her mouth when she smiled. The softness of her lips. He would have liked to hold her one more time, but it wasn't to be. There was no way to stop what he'd set in motion.

He turned from the window and crossed the highly polished wood floor to his desk. The richness of his surroundings provided a comforting reassurance. He glanced at the Newtonian toy that sat on his desk. A row of polished steel balls hung in a row from invisible wires. He reached out and lifted the end ball, then let it fall. The sphere descended, colliding with the next in line, setting in motion a chain reaction through the line of planet-like orbs.

CHAPTER TWO
Three Months Earlier

Aʀɪ Bᴇɴ Lᴇᴠ scrutinized the printout of the scientific model he'd created. His eyes scanned the numbers, searching for his mistake. *Where had he gone wrong?* Everything seemed correct. The results told him otherwise.

One more failure in an endless string of failures. After all those years of trial and error one would have thought he'd be used to the feeling of failure. He wasn't. The letdown was devastating. This time he'd been certain he'd found the solution. How many times had he believed his own words? Too many to count.

"You're a fraud," he admitted to the empty office. Everyone had expected greatness from him: his parents, his teachers, Hannah. He'd let them all down.

All his adult life he'd been searching for the solution to his country's biggest problem: energy. To survive, Israel needed to import ninety-nine percent of its oil and gas. The hunt for energy self-sufficiency had been ongoing since the country's creation in '48. Solar energy provided a third of the country's hot water, but carbon-burning fuels were still king. Prices were continually rising and, owing to the ever-changing political winds, new suppliers continually had to be found. Norway and Mexico had replaced Iran. Resources came in from South Africa and Colombia and a shaky peace had enabled Egyptian gas to join the precarious supplier matrix. But at a moment's notice, any of these nations could refuse to honor their agreements.

Israel had learned to make drinking water from seawater, to turn deserts into green farmland. However, until they were able to discover the miracle of energy self-sufficiency, they were vulnerable. Tanks and planes still ran on the black stuff.

New drilling, development of synthetic substitutes, solar and alternative energies, and improvement in electrical and battery power were continually being explored. None had met with much success. Ari believed the answer lay in fuel cells: low pollution devices generating electrical currents from chemical reactions. Scientists had been working on the technology for generations without any major breakthrough. Ari was certain they'd been following the wrong path.

Existing technology relied on the production of hydrogen for later conversion into electricity. The process required a reformer, a rather large piece of equipment, and a place to store the gas until it was needed. What he was working on was a way to produce hydrogen on demand, eliminating the need for storage and enabling the reformer to come way down in size. His approach was unorthodox. It rejected the conventional wisdom of the day. The concept was brilliant! The only problem, as he reviewed the pages before him, was that it didn't work.

Perhaps they were right, he thought, silently condemning his latest effort. If everyone else saw things differently, perhaps it was time to consider the possibility that they knew something he didn't.

Perhaps he was guilty of the intellectual arrogance his colleagues accused him of. Then again, original thinking had always been a crime. The revelation that the earth revolved around the sun and not the other way around had gotten its early heralds burned at the stake. Even quantum physics, which was now taught like religion, had originally been regarded as quackery.

He wasn't wrong! And yet the numbers on the pages before him didn't lie. He put down the pages and shut his eyes to the scientific model he'd created. *Months of work wasted!* Mortality pressed down upon him. He had wanted to leave something behind other than the son he adored. His legacy would be failure.

Ari opened his eyes. The rows of numbers stared mockingly up at him. He grabbed the offending page and crushed it beneath his fingers, it didn't deserve the life he'd given it. The crumpled ball rolled from his fingers into the basket beside his desk. He reached for the next page. He was ready to impose the same punishment when something caught his eye. His hand froze as he read the numbers before him. Slowly, he picked up the page. His heart raced. He reached down and retrieved the discarded page from the trash, straightening it out before him.

How could he have missed it? The simple mistake was so obvious!

Feverishly, he went through the pages, scribbling notes in the margins, crossing out numbers and replacing them with new ones. Time ceased to exist. He continued on, shifting position when the muscles in his legs demanded

When he finished he put down his pencil.

Only a handful of people in the world had the ability to make sense of what lay before him. Sidney Taylor was one of them. He stopped himself from calling her. It was way too dangerous. In eleven days they would be together at the energy conference in Washington. He would wait till then.

The sharp ringing of the phone invaded his privacy.

"Shalom," Ari said gruffly. His *hello* broadcast no welcome.

"I'm sorry to disturb you," Hannah apologized, knowing her husband didn't appreciate her calls at work.

"It's not a good time," Ari replied, guiltily erasing Sidney from his thoughts.

"I'm sorry, but it's important."

"What is it?" He made no effort to hide his annoyance.

"David's had an accident."

The world stopped.

"He's fine," Hannah assured into the silence. "Just shaken up."

Ari's heart resumed beating.

"What happened?"

"Promise me you're not going to get upset."

"Hannah, for the love of God —"

"He was playing. A boy ran into him in the schoolyard. David fell backwards and hit his head on the pavement."

"Are you sure he's okay?"

"He's fine, just shaken up. We're in the nurse's office at the school."

"He could have a concussion."

"The nurse doesn't think so but I'm taking him to the doctor's just to be safe."

"Is there any slurring of his speech?"

"No."

"Drowsiness? Headache?"

"No, but there's quite a bump on the back of his head."

"Let me speak to him," Ari demanded.

There was no use arguing with her husband. Hannah handed the phone to her son. David answered his father's questions then handed the phone back to his mother.

"He sounds okay," Ari conceded.

"He is."

"What about the boy who pushed him? What's the school going to do to him?"

"They're hanging him in the morning," Hannah replied.

Ari didn't laugh.

"For God's sake, he's a little boy, David's age. They were just playing."

"He could have killed him!"

Hannah didn't reply.

"Do you want me to meet you at the doctor's?"

"There's no reason for that, he's fine. Go have lunch and I'll call you later."

Lunch! Ari checked the clock on the wall. Jacob Barkan, who didn't share Ari's problem with time, would be waiting for him downstairs, probably had been for the last ten minutes.

* * *

"Sorry," Ari said as he descended the stairs.

Jacob Barkan looked up from the book he was reading. He stood waiting at the bottom of the stone staircase that led from the building's lobby to the upper floors. He marked the page and closed the book. He shook his head at Ari disapprovingly.

"Why should this day be different from all others?"

"Sorry. I was on the phone with Hannah, David's had an accident at school," Ari said, guiltily. It was the truth but not the reason for his lateness. Jacob was his best friend, in reality his only real friend, but sometimes even friends told small lies to one another.

"He's all right?" Jacob asked. He loved the boy and worried about him as if he were his own. He and his wife had never been able to have a child. It was a contributing reason though not the only one for their split.

"He's okay. Some kid ran into him and knocked him down."

"But he's all right?"

"He's got a bump on the back of his head, but other than that Hannah said he's fine."

Jacob was relieved to hear it. He checked his watch. He didn't have a class for another hour; Ari's schedule was different. He might show up late for lunch, but he never missed a minute of work.

"I guess that's it for Abdullah's," Jacob said with disappointment. He'd been looking forward to eating at the small Arab restaurant all week; nobody prepared fish with fresh dates better than Abdullah's. The problem was that the restaurant was in the Arab quarter, a good ten-minute walk from where they were.

What the hell, Ari thought, he had reason to celebrate. He'd waited a lifetime for his discovery, fifteen minutes more or less wouldn't change anything. "Let's go," he said, leading the way. "It's my treat, for keeping you waiting."

Jacob hurried to catch up. The change in Ari didn't go unnoticed by Jacob Barkan, very little did.

Jacob taught in the school that occupied the first two floors of the three-story building on Solomon Street. Ari's work was on the top floor, access denied to all but a specific few.

The building itself was nondescript and void of any architectural detail. Essentially, it was a plain rectangular box. As required of all buildings in the city, however, it was faced with Jerusalem limestone from the surrounding Judean Hills. The uniformity made buildings such as this disappear into sameness. The result was that one could easily pass by without ever really seeing it.

The inscription above the entrance identified the place in both Hebrew and English as the "Immigrant Language Immersion Center." It was here, on the first two floors, where newly arrived Jews immigrating from all corners of the world were offered an intensive three-month training course in their new country's language and customs, courtesy of the Israeli government. Every day, a mixture of people, speaking, dressing, and physically looking nothing like one another, passed through these doors. The top floor held something quite different.

A small plaque by the building's entrance bore the name Ergoden, a respected high-tech Israeli corporation that developed highly sophisticated software for companies in the energy industry. The name was Greek, *the path of energy*, an inside joke by the people who created the company. There were several listings for the firm in the phone book but none at this particular address.

Only those who worked on the third floor and a handful of others with the proper clearance were permitted to ascend those steps. At the top of the landing an armed guard checked IDs. Access through the doors beyond could only be achieved by pressing the proper sequence of numbers on the attached security pad. The proprietary nature of the work performed for Ergoden's industrial and governmental clients was the reason given to those who questioned the tight security, but this facility had nothing to do with the daily business for which Ergoden had become known.

To Ari, such security measures were excessive. The Israeli government felt differently. He and others like him were part of the most important military undertaking since Israel's struggle to develop the bomb. Unlike that effort, which had required remote bases buried deep in the Negev Desert, this one was hidden in innocuous looking buildings in civilian areas. The research these people did posed no danger to population centers, and the advances in computer technology made it unnecessary to concentrate the work in any one location.

Sharing space with a school where students barely understood the language, and where they moved on by the time they did, had been someone's idea of pure genius.

In the beginning, Jacob and Ari had passed each other every morning, nodding hello, on the way to their respective workplaces. Nods eventually gave way to conversation, shared interests to friendship.

Jacob Barkan had become as dear to Ari as the brother he'd lost in Lebanon, but still he didn't dare confide the true nature of his work to him. He had come close on several occasions, but had always pulled back at the last moment. Now, more than ever, he wanted to tell him the truth. This was the biggest moment in his life and he wanted to share it.

CHAPTER THREE

THE red Fiat lurched forward with a jerking motion and almost stalled. A puff of black smoke spewed from its exhaust. Yousef felt his heart screech to a halt. A car horn scolded him from behind.

As if it were his fault the vehicle hadn't been maintained. Obviously, those in charge hadn't thought it necessary, given its final destination.

He stole a quick glance behind him at the suitcases on the back seat. Rings of sweat were spreading under his arms. The same car horn blared in a machine-gun staccato. Yousef cursed in Arabic. He pumped the gas pedal. The exhaust crackled like small fireworks and the car inched forward.

He didn't really want to die, not for the promise of sixty virgins, not for a hundred. Yesterday he'd celebrated his twenty-second birthday at his parents' house in Ramallah. The next time he saw his mother and father would be with Allah. His thoughts turned to Kahlil. His brother would have been sixteen next month. The Israelis had murdered him. Shot him for throwing rocks. *Bullets against rocks!* The memory of his mother's cries hardened his will. *Kahlil's death would be avenged. They would cry for their children as his parents had cried for Kahlil.*

It was an honor to be chosen, he told himself. An honor to be martyred for the cause. Allah would reward him.

Yousef glanced back at the suitcases and 150 pounds of explosives they held. His resolve returned as he rejoined the stream of traffic heading into Jerusalem.

"*Sheket!* Children, *be quiet,*" the teacher called out through the cacophony of high-pitched, shrieking voices that swarmed and buzzed within the school bus. "Nathan, sit down! Rachel, stop yelling. Daniel, that means you too!"

It had been a typical class trip and everyone had enjoyed the departure from the daily class routine. The tour of the Knesset, Israel's Parliament, had been a great success. Now, heading back to school, she was grateful it was almost over.

"Miss Levy," a little boy of nine called out as he ran to her, his milk-white cheeks tear-stained. A black ribbon, a symbol of grief and loss, had been pinned to his gray school jacket by his father.

She was about to reprimand the boy for leaving his seat while the bus was moving, then changed her mind. "What is it, Alex?"

Large dark eyes, swollen by sorrow, looked up at her. He didn't answer, he couldn't. If he tried to speak he knew he'd be unable to hold back the tears. They were all watching, he could hear their muffled voices and anticipate their laughter.

He was a child who had learned the unfairness of life. His mother was dead. There had been nothing the doctors could do to stop the cancer. He had watched her shrink, had heard her suffering. Now, with her gone, almost anything set off his tears. His classmates, who had little patience with his crying, teased him relentlessly.

"What is it?" She, too, was losing patience.

"Moshe keeps hitting me."

"Go back and tell him to stop," she instructed.

"I did. He wont' listen. Everyone's laughing, they think it's funny."

Tears overflowed their restraints. Pockets of laughter rose behind him.

Angrily, Miss Levy rose from her seat.

"We'll see about that!" she said. Her voice rose above those of the children's. The bus fell silent.

Taking the boy by the hand, she braced herself against the vehicle's movement and proceeded down the aisle.

After the partition of Palestine in '48, the Arab quarter had been closed to Jews. Synagogues were destroyed, religious sites vandalized. The Jewish cemetery at the Mount of Olives had been desecrated, the headstones used for flooring in public toilets. The city had been reunited following the '67 war and made the capital of Israel, but the old quarter was still mostly Arab.

Church bells tolled and the *muezzin* called the faithful to prayer. Ari Ben Lev and Jacob Barkan finished their lunch at Abdullah's, a small family restaurant in the city that King David made his capital some 3,000 years ago. A city that had not known peace since that time.

The skeletal structure of the fish, with its tail and head still attached, was all that remained on the serving dish. Jacob scraped the last of the sweet sauce onto his spoon and brought it to his lips.

All through lunch the only thing Ari could think about was what he'd left behind at his office. He ached to get back to work, to begin the testing. Jacob kept talking but Ari wasn't really listening. *He'd done it!* Jointed the ranks of Pasteur and Salk. He'd cured the disease of poverty. No more third world countries begging for fuel. There would be enough energy for everyone. He would be hailed as the savior of his country. The Arabs would be furious, no more American Dollars. *Fuck them.*

"So what's this brilliant discovery of yours that's 'going to change the world?'" Jacob asked, licking his spoon before returning it to his plate.

Whether it was the wine or the overwhelming desire to share his triumph, Ari had come dangerously close to putting everything he'd worked for in jeopardy. He checked himself. The near plunge into the reality of what he had done brought him back from the brink.

"Just something I'm working on for a client of ours," Ari replied.

"You said it was going to win you the Nobel prize."

"I was joking."

"No you weren't."

"Do us both a favor and forget I mentioned anything."

"Why?"

"Because I'm not supposed to tell tales out of school, it could cost me my job." It wasn't his job that worried him; it was the possibility of spending the next 20 years in prison.

"Come on," Jacob coaxed, "I'm not going to tell anyone."

Ari hesitated, but before he could answer, the younger of the owner's sons, a boy of about seventeen, approached them and placed their check on the table. There was neither warmth nor a smile from the boy.

Ari reached for the check. The urge to tell all had passed. The boy had unintentionally saved him from a huge mistake.

"Please tell your father the fish was wonderful," Ari said.

May you choke on it, the boy thought as he left them. Unlike his father he resented serving Jews. *One day they'd all be gone, he told himself.* Until then, as a dutiful son, he did what was expected of him.

Forty meters separated Yousef's car from the school bus. It was coming in his direction, slowing to make the turn into the entrance of the school. The guard was in the process of pushing open the tall iron gates. It was good fortune, but not part of the plan. He'd been instructed to drive the bomb right up to the building, but who knew if he'd make it through the gates. The daughter of Lieutenant General Ariel Mizrachi attended the school, and with any luck she was on the bus. Yousef thought of his brother. An eye for an eye.

There was no one to ask for approval, the decision was his alone. In a few moments the bus would disappear behind the gates and the gift that Allah had given him would be lost. He pressed down hard on the accelerator. His hand brushed aside the newspaper that covered the detonator. The Fiat backfired. It belched smoke but continued to race forward.

The guard turned. His hand fell to the Uzi which hung from the strap around his neck.

The bus started its turn. Yousef hammered his foot down on the gas. The Fiat shot forward.

The bus driver looked out in horror at the speeding red car that was coming straight for him. He pushed the pedal to the floor. The heavy bus strained to get out of the way but its response was slow.

"God is great!" Yousef screamed above the report of gunshots. His fingers pressed the detonator.

* * *

Ari was in the doorway of the restaurant when the bomb exploded. Jacob pushed past him and looked above the buildings. In the distance a thick black cloud was spreading, turning day into night. The scream of the sirens began, a precursor to those of the dying.

Throughout the quarter, doors were being closed and locked, shades drawn, windows shuttered. It was not violent reprisals that were feared by the Arab population, but guilt by association. Abdullah and his family were Israeli citizens, but they were also Palestinians. They had voted in the last election, and, in theory, were entitled to equal rights. But whenever the terror struck, all were suspect. They became the enemy.

Abdullah's oldest son hurried to place the "Closed" sign in the window. He drew the curtain. The youngest son stopped clearing the tables. As he did, a smile passed his lips.

CHAPTER FOUR

At a distance, the small village was indistinguishable from the hundreds of others throughout the region. A random assemblage of roughly hewn stone and mud houses of indeterminable age appeared to have grown from the parched, yellow-brown soil of the hillsides. Below the village, scattered clusters of ancient olive trees were carefully maintained. Here and there goats moved lazily about.

As one got closer, however, the resemblance to other villages ended. Dug into the quiet surrounding hillsides, at strategic points, commanding the approach road below, were fortified positions and heavy artillery. In the town, armed men moved about. Stockpiled within the buildings were enough munitions and supplies to start a small war. The village served as the headquarters of The Sword of God.

"Do you have any idea of the damage you've done!?" Abud Rachman raged, unable to control his anger.

Jabal Hussein stood silent and unbending in the room that served as Rachman's headquarters. A small lizard scampered along the dirt floor, gently stirring the dust. Jabal brought his foot down. The stain spread under his boot.

Rachman stood impatiently, waiting for a response. A map of the region hung on the wall behind him. The letters that identified Israel had been blackened out.

Jabal's eyes moved from the map to the face of the man for whom he'd sworn allegiance. He chose to remain silent.

"Your actions serve only to aid our enemy," Rachman said, tightening his grip on the edge of the wooden table that separated them.

"It's not our actions but our unwillingness to act that aids our enemies." Jabal refused to be lectured to by a man who no longer possessed the stomach to lead.

"Silence!" Rachman ordered.

Iradj Bin Rab stood off to one side watching the growing storm. His job was to articulate the organization's politics in ways that the western world found acceptable. Jabal's recent action had complicated things, but, as he valued his throat, he didn't express the sentiment openly. Jabal was no one he wanted for an enemy.

Bin Rab was as comfortable with Western mannerisms and attire as he was with his own. Educated in London, he spoke English with a British accent, understood the mentality of the enemy, and could move between both camps with an ease that was invaluable to the organization. Unlike Jabal, his weapons were words and public opinion. He'd been ordered here by Rachman as a reluctant witness to the unfolding drama. He'd have preferred to be almost anywhere else. Jabal, thankfully, took no notice of him.

Like Rachman, Jabal had come out of the camps and known loss. Both were comfortable with the sword and had used it mercilessly. The similarities ended there. Rachman's beard was streaked with gray, Jabal's was still jet-black. The color was a metaphor for how each saw life. There were no grays for Jabal, he saw everything with the certainty of youth. He'd come up the ranks fast and ruthlessly. Those who opposed him had disappeared along with their opposition. Until recently, however, he'd been fanatically loyal to Rachman, whose name was synonymous with The Sword of God. That was changing. Rachman still spoke for the organization he'd brought into existence but his voice was no longer absolute, and everyone knew it.

Bin Rab watched as disciple and mentor faced off against one another. The threads that had once bound them were frayed. Rachman's gun sat on the table. For a moment Iradj thought Rachman might use it. Under the right circumstances, he might have found such a scenario interesting but not now, not while he was in the line of fire.

"Twenty-nine children dead!"

"Twenty-nine that will never be soldiers facing our people."

"World opinion doesn't see it that way."

"I care nothing for world opinion."

Rachman brought his hand down on the desk. The gun rattled against the wood. "Then you're a fool!"

Jabal's face flushed red, he fought to control his anger.

"I leave world opinion to Bin Rab, it's his job. Mine is to strike our enemies, to kill those who oppress our people," Jabal spat.

"Save the speeches for your followers."

"I seek no followers, only the return of our lands! But if people choose to follow me then perhaps it's because they seek someone to lead." He wasn't ready to challenge Rachman openly but every word reverberated a threat.

Rachman, too, struggled to control his anger. "Do you think you'll get our land back by killing children?"

"We certainly won't get it through negotiation." The word was meant to insult.

"Negotiation is a tool like the sword," Rachman lectured, recalling when he, like Jabal, had allowed hatred to rule his decisions.

"Negotiation." Jabal spat on the ground, ridding his mouth of the aftertaste of the word. "I go down on my knees only to Allah."

Neither Jabal nor Iradj Bin Rab caught the incendiary flash in Rachman's eyes; it appeared and disappeared in an instant.

"There is a season for all things, a time for war and a time for statesmanship. Yesterday the Israelis were willing to talk. Today, they want blood."

"Good!" Jabal said. "It's foolishness to believe it can be otherwise."

Rachman was through trying to reason. They were moving further and further apart. He turned from Jabal to Iradj Bin Rab.

"When do you leave for Paris?"

"In two hours."

"Good. At the press conference you will issue a statement denying any knowledge or involvement by The Sword of God in the bombing."

Jabal started to protest. Rachman silenced him.

"You will initiate no future action without my direct approval. Is that understood?" He leaned on the table, his hand by the gun. He had no desire to start a civil war within the organization, but he'd put a bullet in Jabal's head if he had to.

"As commander of our defense forces I'm responsible —"

"You're responsible to me, and to the organization," Rachman said. "Or do you question that authority as well?"

It wasn't quite time to challenge Rachman's leadership. That time, however, was fast approaching. Jabal struggled to hold his tongue but couldn't. "No man is indispensable."

"I would remember that if I were you," Rachman replied.

CHAPTER FIVE

Rue de Gravan was a quiet, residential, tree-lined street on the left bank of Paris. The limbs of the trees had been dramatically cut back, leaving burly knobs, which in the spring would sprout a topiary ball of green. For the time being, they looked barren and scarred against the gray sky. In the middle of the block, nestled between a small pharmacy and a café whose tables spread along the sidewalk when the weather permitted, stood a narrow building of gray stone. The windows were long and ornately framed, typical of their eighteenth-century construction, but the electronics that protected them were the most up-to-date money could buy. The building housed the political offices of The Sword of God.

The neighbors were not pleased with the building's current occupants but could do nothing about it. France permitted the organization residence within its borders as long as it caused no trouble on French soil. To assure it didn't, the police officially monitored the comings and goings of visitors. Unofficially, the clandestine service of several foreign nations also kept an eye on the building. The watchdogs knew one another and the whole process had taken the air of a game. From time-to-time cups of coffee would be anonymously delivered to the occupants of parked cars.

Inside the building a winding baroque staircase led to offices on the upper floors. Entry to the top floors was strictly forbidden to the public. For today's event the reception hall on the first floor was packed. The folding chairs were long since taken up by early comers. Reporters lined the walls. Others stood by the doors, trying to edge their way in. The room echoed with a cacophony of voices anxious to devour the man addressing them.

The profusion of lights focused on Bin Rab caused tiny beads of perspiration to appear on his forehead. He wiped them away with the back of his hand. Anyone who interpreted the action as a sign of nervousness was mistaken. Standing in front of the cluster of microphones Bin Rab felt completely at ease, victorious in his English-tailored dark blue suit. The voices of the reporters fighting to be heard sounded like the clucking of chickens to Bin Rab. He had thrown out kernels for them to feed upon and now watched with amusement as they fought over them.

"Another child died this morning," a man called out, attempting to be heard. "That makes the death count thirty."

"The death of every child is a tragedy," Iradj replied.

"Then do you condemn the recent bombing?"

"I condemn injustice. However, as I just said, the death of every child is a tragedy and that includes the murder of a Palestinian youth who was shot by Israeli forces this morning protesting the illegal occupation of our lands."

"Surely you're not equating the two incidents!"

Iradj leaned closer to the microphones.

"Is a child's life less important because he's Arab?" He understood how to work his audience.

"As I made clear in my statement, The Sword of God condemns all such wanton acts of violence. However, such reprisals are a direct consequence of the wrongs done to our people. They are inevitable." Voices from the audience ignited, straining to be heard, demanding clarification. His words had created a storm of protest. He waited for the noise to die down before continuing.

"When everything is taken from a people, and frustration is all that's left to fill the vacuum created by the absence of justice, retribution is the inevitable consequence."

"Do you maintain The Sword of God played no part in the bombing?" a reporter for one of the major Paris dailies asked, springing to his feet.

"None whatsoever," Iradj replied. "Though I'm sure some would like to blame us for all violence in that part of the world."

Cameras continued to roll, the chickens clucked louder.

"Would you care to comment on the rumor that serious dissension exists within the leadership of The Sword of God," a man leaning against a sidewall called out.

Iradj hadn't expected the question; neither had anyone else. All eyes were now focused on Iradj, leaving him no choice but to reply.

"Our enemies would like you to think that was so, but nothing could be further from the truth. We are one voice and one leader: Abud Rachman," Iradj replied.

"Then there's no truth that there's a struggle for power by some of the more radical elements of your organization?" The troublemaker refused to let go.

"I believe I just answered that question." Iradj was not pleased with the direction the news conference had taken. Nor was he pleased that someone in his organization had leaked information.

"Next question," he said, searching the crowd for a friendlier face. He found it in a young woman. She was American, with a midwestern, scrubbed-clean look. Her blond hair was tied tightly back, her hand was raised. The motion caused the jacket of her suit to open, revealing the soft cream-colored silk blouse.

"Miss Gordon."

"With regard to the bombing of a school bus, does The Sword of God consider such an attack an act of terrorism?"

"It's important to remember that the term terrorist is usually applied by those who subjugate to those who would fight against them for freedom. When the Israelis fought the British, the English called them terrorists. Now that Israel has taken over its oppressor's mantle, they label us as the terrorists."

"But surely the killing of innocents —"

"How many innocents has your country killed in Vietnam? In Panama, Kosova and now in Afghanistan and Iraq?"

"We don't target children."

"Neither do we. But in war, innocents fall victim." It was time for him to practice the rhetoric in which he'd become so well rehearsed. "The Israelis must be made to see that their own actions encourage such tragedies. They must ask themselves where and with whom the ultimate responsibility lies for the death of those children."

Voices rose in outrage. Iradj Bin Rab spoke loudly into the microphone drowning out the dissent.

"I bring you assurances from Abud Rachman that The Sword of God was in no way responsible for yesterday's attack. Furthermore, he extends his personal sympathy to the victims and their parents and hopes the voices of those who now mourn will rise up to insist that their leaders end this senseless bloodshed."

The fox had routed the chickens and confusion raged. Iradj put up his hand commanding order.

"I also remind you that Abud Rachman's childhood was spent in the refugee camps. He's seen the suffering and death of those whom he loved. And still, he seeks an end to the violence, and a fair and peaceful solution to his people's conflict. He offers Israel the olive branch or the gun. The choice is theirs. But to those who'd chose the gun and who would continue to repress the legitimate rights of our people he issues this warning: The Sword of God will continue to *defend* itself. The killing will not stop until the oppressors stop killing our children. There can be no peace without honor and no honor without justice!"

The cameras kept recording as the room broke into an unintelligible mass of raised voices. Iradj Bin Rab had just turned everything upside down. He did his job well. To him, truth and morality were abstracts. Neither held sway in the courts or in the politics of war.

It had been a difficult press conference and a long day. He was grateful it was over. In the privacy of his hotel room he relinquished the mask of invincibility he'd been forced to wear throughout the conference and finally allowed himself to feel tired. He gave thanks to Allah that he was able to function on so little sleep.

Just a short catnap on the plane was all he'd managed. He'd trained himself to operate like this since his days at boarding school. It hadn't been intellect alone that had enabled him to excel above his English classmates. How naive he'd been back then, believing hard work and superior grades would earn him the respect of his fellow students. They quickly reminded him of what he'd forgotten: He was, first-and-foremost, an Arab. Neither his grades nor his parent's money would save him from the prejudices of English society.

He hadn't realized it at the time, but his English classmates had done him a favor. Their ostracism drew him closer towards his roots and the spreading Islamic revolution. By the time he'd graduated, he'd acquired a classical education and a burning contempt for the West. He could walk comfortably in both worlds but trusted only one.

Standing naked in the semidarkness of the bathroom, feeling the cool marble beneath his feet, he finished pissing, then made his way back to the bedroom of his suite. His leg brushed against the cream-colored silk blouse that hung from the arm of a reproduction Louis XIV chair. The blouse slid onto the floor. He didn't bother to pick it up.

He looked down at the face of the American reporter who slept so peacefully. The streetlight that filtered through the partially draped window illuminated her white skin. He sat down on the edge of the bed and gathered in his hand the golden strands from off the pillow. He let them slide through his fingers.

Her eyes slowly opened. They focused on him. She smiled. Her hand reached for his and brought his fingers to her lips. She pulled him towards her.

He knew she was the enemy, Paris's Helen, and yet, he went willingly.

CHAPTER SIX

Have you remembered everything?" Hannah asked, fashioning the belt of her bathrobe into a bow that tightened around her waist.

Ari silently struggled with the zipper of his suitcase. It was stuck. He tried forcing it without success. The bed, giving way to his frustration, rocked with the effort.

"Damn!"

"Here, let me do that for you," Hannah said, brushing past him. Men were like small boys to her, always needing help.

"I can do it myself!" He yanked the zipper back and the teeth gave up their hold on the caught material. Reversing direction, he pushed down on the clothing and worked the zipper back around.

"Do you have the list?" Hannah asked.

"In my wallet." He despised her lists. Every time he traveled she gave him one. He spent half his free time running around, shopping for her.

"Check to make sure," Hannah said. He glanced at her but didn't answer.

Her constant mothering made being with Sidney all the more appealing.

"Just check," she insisted, reaching for the pocket where he kept his wallet.

He grabbed her hand. Startled, she stared at him. He released his grip, then took the wallet from his pocket and withdrew the list to show her. "There! Satisfied?"

"What in the world's gotten into you?" Hannah asked.

"Nothing, just stop treating me like a child. I'm not David."

"Asking you to check is treating you like a child?"

Where the hell was Jacob? He'd promised to drive him to the airport.

"I don't want to fight," Ari said.

"Neither do I. I was just trying to help."

"Sometimes I just prefer to do things myself." He locked the suitcase and lifted it off the bed, then picked up his coat.

"Remember to call when you get to the hotel."

She was doing it again! This time he didn't react. What was the use? It wasn't her, it was he who had changed.

He felt her eyes, but didn't dare meet them as he exited the bedroom. She followed him into the hallway.

"We need to talk."

"Not now," he replied.

"Yes, now!"

He stopped, unwillingly put down his bag, laid his coat on top, and turned to face her.

"Jacob's going to be here any minute."

"He can wait a few minutes."

"Hannah —"

"Why are you so unwilling to talk to me?"

She was right. He'd been avoiding her ever since the thing with Sidney started.

"Is it me? Something I've done?" Hannah asked.

"No."

"Then what? It seems I can't speak to you any more without you blowing up."

She was right. In some perverse way he blamed her for the lies he was forced to tell her. It was unfair and it had to stop.

"I'm sorry," Ari apologized. "It's been a little tense at work lately. There may be some changes, people may be losing their jobs. I didn't mean to take it out on you."

"Are you in any danger?" she asked.

He sensed the worry his lie evoked.

"No." *He needed to put an end to the lies.* He would, he promised himself, when he got back.

She hugged him and patted his back reassuringly, the same way she comforted David when he was feeling bad.

It couldn't go on like this. He was making both of them miserable. He loved her, just not the way he loved Sidney.

He kissed her goodbye then released himself from her arms. "I'd better get going." He picked up his coat and slipped it on.

"Did you remember to pack your gloves? It can be cold this time of year in Washington."

Ari patted the pocket of his coat. "I'll be right back," he said and moved down the hall to his son's room.

"Don't wake him, it's too early for him to get up."

Silently, Ari slipped into David's room. The boy lay beneath the blankets, curled up in his bed, the cover tucked under his chin. Ari sat down on the edge of the bed. He brushed the hair off David's forehead and planted a kiss. The boy's eyes opened a crack.

"Is it time for school?"

"No. I'm leaving for the airport, just wanted to say goodbye. How's the bump?"

"Still hurts."

"I love you," Ari whispered.

David breathed in deeply and closed his eyes. "Bye Daddy," he murmured.

Ari kissed him again then quietly crossed to the bedroom door.

"Bring me a present from America," David called, his large dark eyes fixed on his father. They were Hannah's eyes.

"We'll see. Depends on the report I get from your mother."

"I'll be good," David promised.

"Go back to sleep." The instruction wasn't necessary, David's head was already back on the pillow, his eyes closed. Ari left the room, quietly closing the door behind him

"You spoil that child," Hannah chided with a smile.

"Oh, and I suppose you don't?" Their love for David was the constant they still shared.

The buzzer downstairs rang twice.

"That's Jacob."

Ari quickly retrieved his bag. Hannah walked him to the door of their apartment, they kissed goodbye.

She waited in the empty doorway listening as his footsteps descended the stairs. When they grew faint she locked the door and went to the living room window. It looked down onto the street below. Jacob's car sat double-parked, a blue smoke spewing from the exhaust.

She watched Jacob put Ari's suitcase in the back seat. He closed the door and walked around to the driver's side. A moment later the car drove off. Never once did Ari look up. Never had he searched to see if she was standing by the window waiting to wave a final goodbye.

His departure left her with an uneasiness she couldn't explain. He had changed. Perhaps it was the work but she feared something else: the approach of middle age, the season when men were known to question their lives and do stupid things.

They'd met at the university. Back then his star had burned brightly. He was determined to shake the world, become a famous scientist. It was a lifetime ago, a time when she still dreamed of becoming a great violinist. Back then everything was possible. Back then her skin was smooth and men still vied for her attention.

The years had passed. The future Ari had painted for them never materialized. His scientific genius never quite flowered and the promises he'd made to her remained unfulfilled. *It didn't matter to her. Why was it so hard for him to understand that?* She'd forgiven him his ambition, but it seemed impossible for him to forgive himself. If there were problems between them, she blamed herself for her fear to confront them. She stood transfixed by the window, looking down at the spot where Jacob's car had stood. *He was a good friend, to all of them.*

The ride to Ben Gurion Airport was strained. Ari had driven most of the way barely speaking. The incident with Hannah was still working on him. The only other subjects he really wanted to talk about were Sidney and his work, and neither of those could he discuss openly with Jacob.

He glanced out his window. A pickup truck loaded with Arab workers was passing in the opposite direction. A young, dark-skinned man, holding fast to the side of the truck to keep himself from falling out, stared back at him in defiance. Their eyes met for a moment and then he was gone.

Ari couldn't wait to leave it all behind: to get aboard the plane that would deliver him to Sidney. With Sidney there was no weight of judgment or residue of failure, she accepted him as he was. He had thought of telling Hannah of his discovery, but decided against it. For what purpose? To justify a lifetime of missed promises? What did it matter, he was destined to disappoint her, anyway — far worse this time than ever before. He was in love with someone else, and he was tired of living a lie.

There were still weeks, if not months of work ahead of him. He was certain he'd found what he'd been searching for. But what if he were wrong this time as well? The question had justified his keeping the discovery from his boss. He would report his findings when he could confirm them. As for Jacob, he would tell him everything, when the time was right.

"Care to tell me about it?" Jacob said.

Had Jacob read his thoughts? He turned from the window to look at him.

"Ever since that day at Abdullah's you've been different," Jacob said. "You've been going around in your own private world, keeping everyone out. You have no time for Hannah or David, let alone me."

"I don't know what you're talking about," Ari replied, defensively.

"You've barely said two words to me the whole way out here."

"I have things on my mind, that's all."

"Care to share them with a friend?"

"It's nothing important," Ari said.

"It has something to do with that discovery you started to tell me about, doesn't it? The one that's going to earn you the Nobel prize."

"I told you, I can't discuss it."

"Can't or won't?"

Why had he ever mentioned it? Because he'd made the discovery of a lifetime and it had been impossible to keep his mouth shut.

"It's proprietary information. I'm not supposed to discuss it outside the office," Ari said.

"Who am I going to tell?"

"It's not that," though Ari knew it was. One slip and Jacob could send them both to prison.

"Fine, forget it!" Jacob said, turning onto the airport road. He had tried his best to get Ari to come clean. He knew him well enough to know it would be a mistake to push further. He let the subject drop, and the two of them drove the rest of the way in a mutually uncomfortable silence.

Inside the terminal they barely spoke as they made their way through the crush of travelers. Businessmen, tourists, pilgrims, and people seeing off friends and relatives pushed by them, trying to gain inches. The loudspeaker continually blared messages in a variety of languages. The crush of humanity was exacerbated by the airport's tight security. Ben Gurion was the only international airport in Israel. Flights from around the world came and went through this singular port. To the Israelis' credit there hadn't been a terrorist incident at the airport in over 40 years.

"Don't be angry with me," Ari said as they reached the screening point. "I promise, once I can speak about it you'll be the first to know." Jacob didn't answer.

"Still friends?" Ari said, holding out his hand. Jacob took it.

"Sure. Only, trust me a little bit more."

"I trust you with my life, with David's and Hannah's," Ari said. He gave Jacob an affectionate hug.

"You'd better get going," Jacob said. "I'll pick you up when you get back."

"If it's a problem, I'll take a taxi."

'I'll be here," Jacob assured.

The loudspeaker announced the boarding call for Ari's plane. They parted and Ari headed for his gate. He stopped, turned, and waved before disappearing into the moving crowd.

Jacob reached into the pocket of his coat and took out his cell phone. He punched in the appropriate numbers. After several rings, a voice answered.

"Barkan here," Jacob said. "He's getting on the plane now. Notify Washington he's on the way."

CHAPTER SEVEN

T HE takeoff from Israel was delayed three hours. From New York, poor weather conditions in the Washington area had further delayed Ari's arrival. By the time he got his luggage, hailed a cab and made it to the hotel, the day was gone and so was the time he'd planned to spend with Sidney. He called her from his room. No one answered. There was nothing to do except finish unpacking, then try to find her.

Ari glanced out through the window. A multitude of lights glowed below him. The city was designed like a wagon wheel, its broad boulevards and avenues radiating from its hub. Monolithic buildings and statuary attested to an empire that touched every part of the world. From his vantage point he could make out the dome of the Capitol Building. Someplace down there was the Lincoln Memorial. He remembered his first impression standing on the granite steps, looking up at Abraham Lincoln carved in white marble. *A new nation conceived in Liberty, and dedicated to the proposition that all men are created equal.* The words had stayed with him, his discovery would add to them.

America was a fantastic country. He marveled at his parents' decision to leave it to struggle in an unforgiving part of the world where people were killed for being Jews. As for himself, he'd grown up in Israel, it was the only home he'd known. The thought of leaving it, like leaving his family, filled him with guilt.

He went back to the bed and picked up the white dress shirts Hannah had carefully ironed for him. Everything he had brought with him could fit comfortably into one drawer of the dresser. *Did Americans really travel with enough clothes to fill all the rest?* The room was nothing special by American standards but for an Israeli it was wonderfully luxurious: deep, thick carpet, a king-sized bed, and a small refrigerator and mini-bar that offered temptations day and night. He took out a small bottle of J&B and poured himself a drink.

The television, tuned to the news, droned in the background. The American president was still pushing his missile defense shield, there had been another suicide bombing in Israel and the weather in Washington was unseasonably cold.

Ari put his remaining things away and relegated the empty suitcase to the closet. He turned off the set and tried Sidney's room again. Still no answer. He left another message. The bed beckoned to him. Sleep would be wonderful but his body needed Sidney. If she was in the hotel he would find her.

* * *

The hotel's bar was packed with people when Ari arrived. His eyes gradually adjusted to the dim light, filling in the shadowed areas with definition. He recognized some people from previous conferences, a few he knew by name, most only by sight. Behind the bar, two men moved like jugglers performing for their audience. Rows of wineglasses hung above their heads. Ari scanned the room for the one person who interested him. He spotted her sitting at a table across the room, waving to catch his attention. The men at her table turned in Ari's direction.

Ari made his way over.

"Ari, good to see you!" Janik Peterson said, rising to his feet and extending his hand. Tall and blond, Peterson was undeniably of Scandinavian origin. He attended the conferences looking for prospects for his search firm. The two other men at the table, Ari assumed, filled the bill.

"You know Sidney, of course."

"We're old friends," Ari said. Sidney offered him her cheek. He kissed her hello, lingering to take in the smell of her perfume. Her skin was warm against his lips.

"Gentlemen," Peterson said, pulling over a chair, "allow me to introduce the celebrated Ari Ben Lev."

"Hardly celebrated," Ari corrected. He'd published a few noteworthy papers on alternative energy and fuel cell technology, but nothing he'd call groundbreaking. They weren't meant to be. His government sent him to these conferences to get information, not to give it.

Peterson continued the introductions: Niels Christensen was from Denmark, Erik Kohl, from Germany. Though they'd never met, Ari was familiar with both their work. Such had certainly been the case when he'd first met Sidney. He'd read her articles in various journals, found her ideas to be original and provoking, but until they were introduced at the conference in Brussels, he'd assumed that Sidney Taylor was a *he*. The revelation came as an awkward but pleasant surprise, as did their mutual attraction

"I read your latest paper," Kohl said. His expertise was fusion. It was also his religion. He merely tolerated other alternative forms of energy. "Your exposition was pleasant reading but surely you can't really believe that fuel cells pose a serious challenge to carbons in our lifetime?"

"I do."

Kohl laughed. "Perhaps, if we live to be a hundred. Right now it's simply not a viable technology." He turned to Sidney for endorsement.

Ari had an instant dislike for the man. It had little to do with his arrogance of his position and everything to do with the way he looked at Sidney.

"You couldn't be more wrong," Ari countered.

"Look, I'm not saying the principle doesn't work, we all know it does, in theory, but in the 160 years since Sir William described the process, no one has yet solved the two underlying problems: size and cost. Until someone does, the science simply isn't practical."

Ari had to keep himself from telling the German that someone was sitting across the table from him.

"No," Kohl went on, "I'm afraid fuel cells are still the unfulfilled promise of dreamers." He turned back to Sidney. "Tell him. You Americans have been using them for over thirty years in your space program at a cost of over six hundred thousand dollars a kilowatt." He laughed.

"Of course, there are phosphoric cells. Significantly less expensive," Kohl said, turning back to Ari, "but at forty-five hundred dollars a kilowatt, still outrageously high. Besides, the darn things are half the size of a railroad car. Compare that to about a thousand dollars per kilowatt of electricity generated from coal, oil or nuclear power and you see the hopelessness of your fuel cell. Now fusion —"

"What if someone could design a cell that provided power for under fifty dollars a kilowatt?" Ari interrupted.

Kohl began to laugh. "He'd own the world! But given the requisite size of the reformer —"

"What if it could be miniaturized?"

Kohl blew air through his teeth. "Not possible."

"Why not? Computer processors used to fill rooms, now they're smaller than your fingernail."

Kohl studied Ari for a moment, then wagged a finger at him. "For a moment I thought you were serious."

"What if I am?"

"Then allow me to recommend a good doctor. We're supposed to be men of science, not science fiction."

"Spoken like a true man of vision," Ari replied. Kohl bristled at the remark.

"Gentlemen," Peterson quickly interjected, trying to defuse the situation. The discussion was endangering his business. "How about another round?"

Sidney declined, she had barely touched the drink in front of her.

"I'm afraid you'll have to excuse me but it's late and I have a long day ahead of me," she said, getting up from her chair.

Ari was the only one not to protest her departure.

"It's still early," Kohl objected.

Unswayed, she bid them goodnight.

The men at the table watched her go. Their interest wasn't strictly professional.

"A most attractive woman," Kohl remarked. Peterson and Christiansen concurred.

"I should be going as well," Ari stated.

"Not you too!" Peterson entreated.

"You forget, I'm still on Israeli time. For me the night's already come and gone."

"I have something I'd hoped to talk to you about," Peterson said. "An offer I think may be of interest to you."

"Tomorrow. Right now the only thing of interest to me is finding my bed. Thanks for the drink."

A man, sitting by himself at a small table, his back against the wall and a half-empty drink before him, stopped doodling on his napkin. His features were Slavic. His nose was flat like a boxer's. It had been broken at some point in his life and the damage never repaired. He'd been at the airport when Ari arrived and had followed him to the hotel. He'd also been there to witness Ari and Sidney's inability to keep their eyes from each other. As Ari passed him, the man put away his pen and followed him out of the bar.

Temporarily Out Of Service. The sign stood before the opened elevator door. A man inside the cab was working on the control panel. By the time the second elevator descended to the lobby a crowd had collected. The door opened and those waiting pushed their way in, barely allowing those inside to get out.

Ari stood before the closing doors. The man who'd followed him out of the bar stood in the rear, his back against the wall. People were packed shoulder to shoulder. Two women, their accents Southern, talked annoyingly loud. Ari focused on the lighted numbers above his head. Each sequential illumination brought him closer to Sidney.

The elevator stopped and the two women got off. Those remaining shared an unspoken relief. The man with the flattened nose maintained his distance from Ari. The elevator ascended, then stopped again. The door opened and Ari exited. The boxer waited until the last possible moment, until the door was about to close.

"Excuse me," he said, pushing by, taking no notice of grunts from the people he elbowed. He grabbed the door, preventing it from closing, and stepped out.

Except for Ari and the boxer, the hallway was empty. The lighting was recessed, the wattage low. Ari stopped before one of the rooms. The boxer closed the distance between them. His hand reached into his jacket pocket and brought something out, concealing it in his palm.

The door before Ari opened. Sidney threw her arms around him.

The boxer pretended to examine the object in his palm as if checking the key-card to his room. He passed by the two lovers and proceeded down the hallway. The pretense wasn't necessary. Ari Ben Lev and the woman were far too interested in each other to take any notice of him. When he heard the door close he turned and headed back towards the elevator, putting the camera back in his pocket.

Ari lay on his side, looking at Sidney. He was tired but didn't want to close his eyes, frightened that if he did the vision next to him might vanish. For the moment he was content just to look at her.

Sidney lay on her back, spent from their lovemaking. She rolled over to face him, their bodies nearly touched. She had been in love before but never like this.

"God, I've missed you," she whispered.

"I love you," he replied.

She'd heard the words before, but they were different coming from him.

As a child, strangers would stop her parents in the street to make a fuss over her. Her father paraded her around as if beauty was a talent and she was expected to perform. *Doors open up for a girl with your looks* her father had constantly reminded her, ignoring her academic achievement. She was always at the top of her class, but it always came down to her looks.

It was her looks that got her noticed by Roger Glass and gave her the edge over her male counterparts. She wished it had been different. Then again, she wished so many things in her life had been different.

Ari moved his body against hers. She felt the warmth of his skin against her own.

"I love you," he whispered, again, his lips searching for the soft skin of her neck.

"Then marry me." The words came out before she realized they were hers. "I'm sorry," she immediately said, but the damage had already been done. Ari pulled back. The spell was broken, paradise lost.

"Don't you think I want to?"

"Sometimes I'm not so sure."

"It's going to happen, only give it time. I can't just pick up from one day to the next and go. I have responsibilities. Things that need to be put in place before I can leave."

"How long am I supposed to wait? A year? Two? Never?"

"You're not being fair," Ari replied, reaching for her.

"Don't!" She moved away and got out of bed. She took her robe from off the chair.

"I'm tired of being fair! I want us to be together."

"We will be."

She slipped her robe on and fastened it around her.

"Come back to bed," Ari said.

"If you're really serious about coming here," Sidney asked, "why won't you let me speak to people who can help you? You could be earning double what they're paying you in Israel."

Something fell into place for Ari. "Peterson said he had something for me, a job, I presume. Did you have anything to do with that?"

"Why would it be so wrong if I did?"

"Because I asked you to wait. I told you, it's not a matter of money. There are things I have to set straight before I can go. It's not just my family, I'm leaving my country." He worked for the Israeli government, but she didn't know that.

"I don't understand this attachment of yours to Israel. All it offers is more fighting and more death."

She wasn't wrong and yet it was still his home. He'd made up his mind to tell her the truth about his work and his discovery, but not now. She was too upset with him, already for delaying his move to America.

"Ever hear of Ramat Gan?" he asked.

"No."

"No reason you should. It's a quiet suburb of Tel Aviv, of no military significance whatsoever. It's where I grew up. During the Gulf War it became Iraq's prime target. Scuds rained down, killing indiscriminately. No one knew if they contained poison gas or biological agents. Parents and children ran to distribution centers to be fitted for gas masks. There weren't enough to go around. People were frantic."

"I don't understand what this has —"

"My parents' building took a direct hit. One moment it was there, the next everything was gone. I lost them both in an instant. My brother died two year later patrolling the Lebanese boarder."

She came over and sat down at the foot of the bed. "I should think after all that you'd be happy to leave that awful place."

"It's not awful," Ari said. "When I was a little boy, I'd ask my parents why they'd immigrated to Israel. They told me they'd gotten tired of living with a packed suitcase under the bed. It was their joke. I didn't understand it at the time. I do now. Israel isn't just a piece of land to Jews, it's a sanctuary. For the last two thousand years the only thing that most nations could agree on was their hatred of us. That kind of unanimity of purpose tends to create a justifiable sense of paranoia amongst my people."

"I don't relish the idea of living there, but I'd move to be with you if it were possible," Sidney said.

Ari knew it wasn't. There was the problem of the language and the culture, and of Sidney finding work. It made more sense for him to come to her.

"I never asked that of you," he said.

"We can go back to visit whenever you want," Sidney offered.

There would be no going back, and Ari knew it. That was what made it so hard.

The phone rang. Sidney glanced at the clock. It was after eleven. She got up, went over to the table by her bed and picked up the receiver. "Hello?"

"Miss me?" The ground beneath her gave way. Her hand moved to her neck, involuntarily pulling together the sides of her robe.

"Are you there?" Roger asked. He was calling from the suite he kept in the city for the times he worked late and didn't make it back to his house and wife in Connecticut. Sidney was *familiar* with it.

"You woke me, I was sleeping."

"Liar," Ari whispered playfully.

The word stung. She covered the mouthpiece of the phone with her hand. *My* boss, she mimed, carrying the phone as far away from the bed as the cord would stretch.

Ari pulled lightly on the cord, attempting to drag her back. Sidney motioned for him to stop.

"You sound different," Roger said.

"You woke me. Is everything okay?" She needed to choose her words carefully.

"Everything's fine. I just called to tell you I miss you." If he expected a response in kind he didn't get it.

"Roger, it's after eleven and I'm exhausted. I'll call you back in the morning."

"I've got an early morning meeting," he said apologetically. "I'll call you as soon as it breaks."

She was obviously angry with him. He hadn't intentionally been ignoring her. Business had been unusually crazy, forcing him to travel far more than usual. He had hoped to make it up to her in Washington, but that hadn't worked out the way he'd planned.

"You know, it wasn't my idea that Elizabeth join me in D.C.," he said.

Sidney was grateful that she had. What would she have done if both he and Ari had shown up at the same time? She needed to end it with Roger, once and for all.

"She insisted on coming," Roger added.

"I understand."

Roger was certain she didn't.

Sidney couldn't deny he'd been good to her. Nor did she want to hurt him. But what had happened between them had been a mistake, it never should have started. *It wasn't love.* For a time she'd convinced herself otherwise, but that was before she understood the difference. She would speak with him when she got back to New York.

"You're angry at me," Roger said.

"No, I'm just tired."

He knew better. Tomorrow he'd have his assistant pick up something at Harry Winston's, a peace offering for not seeing her in Washington.

"Sleep well," Roger said.

"You too." She didn't wait to hear the disconnect. She hung up and placed the phone back on the bedside table. *What a mess she'd made of her life!*

"He thinks his employees have no life outside the company," Sidney said, feeling the need to further explain herself.

Ari held out his hand. She took it and he drew her to him. A tear fell onto the linen sheet, it went unnoticed. Another fell and this time Ari looked up. He misunderstood their source.

"Just a little more time," he promised. "Everything's going to work out. You'll see."

CHAPTER EIGHT

Half a world away from the glitter of Washington, General Alexander Primikov was holding a late-night meeting. His remote dacha was reachable only by a single approach road or through snow-laden woods. The estate had been built for a prince of the Romanoff family, confiscated by a high-ranking member of the Party, and now belonged to the general. Alexander Primikov, though no longer a general, still preferred the title. Yuri Stroeva, the president of Russia, had recently appointed him to the post of Minister of Energy. The appointment, masked as an important government position, had actually been a political neutering of Primikov, an outspoken critic of the present government and a clear danger to President Stroeva's reelection.

Stroeva would have preferred to simply dismiss the general from his position, but the political dangers of such a move were too great. Primikov's popularity had already grown beyond the point where he could be removed without due cause. He was a senior officer who commanded the respect and loyalty of his men. Firing him was a wild card Stroeva didn't care to play.

His appointment to Minister of Energy had been a brilliant chess move on Stroeva's part. It declawed the bear, separating the general from his power base. The new minister could be sent into the recesses of the country and on lengthy missions outside Russia's borders to handle energy-related matters. In this way his influence could be managed and his popularity neutralized.

But Yuri Stroeva had greatly underestimated his opponent. Alexander Primikov was not a man to be easily pushed aside. Just as Joseph Stalin's early rivals attempted to distance him from power by making him head of the regime's then nonexistent security forces,

Stroeva, too, had unwittingly provided his nemesis with the vehicle for his ascension to power.

The guests at the dacha had been there most of the evening, eating and toasting together. Dimitri Danchenko, a successful businessman with extensive holdings throughout Russia, reclined in his high-backed chair at one end of the massive dining room table. His Slavic face was wide, his features coarse. His large hands were unusually strong, capable of breaking a man's neck with little effort. In the years following the fall of Communism, it had not been intellect alone that caused his rise in power and wealth. He listened to a speech he had heard many times before.

"Russia, my friends, has been betrayed!" Heads nodded in unison. Alexander Primikov's hand circled the table. "Look around: We are all that stands between her and ruin. Fail her now, and Russia is finished!" Murmurs of agreement jousted to be heard.

"Once a power to be reckoned with, Russia has become inconsequential under the present leadership, a nation easily dismissed by our enemies. Our greatness squandered while those who really care are forced to watch our homeland bartered away piece by piece!" His voice rose as it had done so often, energizing the disenfranchised victims of the system who supported his ascendancy to power. "Russia will be great again, this I promise you."

As he spoke he studied the reactions of Nina Ranevskaya, the sole woman in their small group. Not yet forty, she already occupied a position of influence on the nation's highest court. Primikov's eyes were continually drawn to her. The other guests were military men, politicians and business people, two of whom were known to have ties to Russian organized crime. For the present, however, Primikov regarded them as necessary evils. He would reevaluate their usefulness later, once he took power.

Outside the dining room, before heavy wooden doors emblazoned with carved animal heads, stood a uniformed soldier. He pretended to hear nothing of what was being said in the room behind him.

"Number three —check in," a voice commanded through the man's headset.

"Position three secure," the soldier replied into the mouthpiece.

One by one, other men positioned around the perimeter of the house and along the approach road reported in. The men, highly trained and loyal soldiers who had served under the general in Afghanistan, believed unflinchingly in his cause. Each could be counted on to give his life, if need be. They maintained ongoing communication with one another and Major Ivan Sobolev, the man responsible for the general's personal safety.

The meeting ended and the heavy wooden doors opened. The guard snapped to attention, letting the guests pass.

"Count on my full support, Alexi," Primikov's opposite in the Russian airforce assured.

"I am," Primikov replied, his hand warmly grasping that of the officer's.

Coats were fetched, cars were brought around, and slowly the group began to thin. Alexander Primikov continued to bid goodnight to his guests. He walked Dimitri Danchenko to the door.

"Dimitri, my friend, I need an answer," Primikov said. "Can I count on you?" He needed the man's money to defeat Stroeva.

"On me, always. But the others require some assurances."

"Is my word not assurance enough?"

"Of course, General. However, you're asking for a considerable sum of money. My associates represent national business interests. They don't wish to see favors being given to the same foreign carrion that Stroeva has allowed to pick the bones of Russian industry."

"You can assure your associates that our interests are one and the same."

"They'll be pleased to hear that." Danchenko tried to read Primikov. There was a lot at stake and he needed to be sure that the general could be trusted, and *controlled*.

"Then I can expect their financial support?" the general asked.

"They have already invested heavily in you."

"Not in me," the general corrected, "in Russia."

"I view it as one and the same, Alexi." The comment pleased Primikov but he would have preferred the assurance of the funds he requested.

"Remind your associates that it's an investment they can't afford not to make."

Danchenko smiled, they were the words he would have chosen had their positions been reversed.

Bidding him goodnight, the general turned his attention to Nina, who was in the process of putting on her coat.

"Nina."

She turned to face him.

"Please stay a few moments more. There's something of importance I need to discuss with you."

She hesitated momentarily, anxious to get home. The weather was frightful and getting worse. The general, however, was not one to be denied. She removed her coat.

When the last guests had gone, Alexander Primikov approached her. She'd been standing patiently, her folded coat in her arms.

"Thank you for waiting, Nina."

"You said it was important."

"It is. Let's go into the other room." The general took her by the arm.

"I really need to be going soon," Nina said. "It's late and it's starting to snow again." It was a long drive back to the city. If the winds picked up, it would be slow and treacherous going.

"I won't keep you long," the general promised.

His private study was large. Heads of wild boar, elk and bear decorated the walls. In the large stone hearth, a fire blazed. Someone had recently added fresh logs to the ones already burning. The flames danced in brilliant reds and oranges. Sparks, like the crackling of fireworks, flew up the chimney.

"Please make yourself comfortable," the general directed.

Nina Ranevskaya sat down on a couch near the fire. She felt the warmth from the flames on her face.

"Can I offer you a drink?" Primikov asked, pouring cognac into a cut-crystal glass. She declined. There was a knock on the door.

"Come in," the general ordered.

A tall, serious-looking man entered.

"Of course you know Major Sobolev."

"Good evening, Major," Nina Ranevskaya said.

Sobolev acknowledged her with a slight nod. His eyes, cold as the air outside the dacha, never left hers.

"The building and grounds are secure, General."

"Very good, Major. That will be all for now." The major saluted and closed the door behind him.

"An excellent man," Primikov said. "Highly dedicated. Extremely efficient. Quite protective of me."

"Alexi, I don't mean to sound ungrateful, but I really must be getting back to Moscow. You said there was something you wanted to talk to me about?"

"Yes, of course." Alexander Primikov took a sip of the cognac and then seated himself on the couch, facing her. "Actually, Major Sobolev is part of what I wanted to discuss with you.

"The Major believes there is a member of our group who has betrayed our trust." Primikov placed the glass on the table before him. He turned back in time to see the red glow on her face turn the color of cold ash.

"This person, I'm told, reports our confidences to Stroeva. So, as a respected and learned magistrate, I thought I'd ask your opinion of how you would judge and sentence such a person."

"I find it hard to believe that one of us — "

"So did I," the general concurred. "That's why I'm asking you directly."

"Me! Surely, Alexi, you're not serious?" It took all her strength to rise to her feet.

"Sit down."

Nina Ranevskaya did as she was told. The general waited patiently for her to speak.

"Alexi," her heart pounded, "Major Sobolev has obviously made certain accusations against me. I tell you now, he is mistaken."

"I'm relieved to hear that, Nina."

"I'm not questioning the Major's motives, but I'm shocked that you, above all people, Alexi, would put weight behind such allegations."

"Then you haven't met with Stroeva?"

She was being judged as she had judged others. It would be a mistake to deny she'd met with the president.

"Yes, I've met with Stroeva on one, no, two occasions. He summoned me. I could hardly have refused to meet with him."

"You never mentioned those meetings to me."

"There was nothing to mention. He asked me for my position on pending legislation, that's all."

"Nothing more than that?"

"If there was, you would have known about it."

"So then Major Sobolev is mistaken?"

"Completely. I would never betray you Alexi."

"I'm relieved to hear that," Primikov said, rising to his feet. He offered her his hand and helped her up.

"It's late, and I've kept you long enough." He walked with her to the door. "You had better get started before the major begins to question my motives for keeping you so long," he said with a disarming smile.

Nina Ranevskaya forced a smile. The general's hands cupped her shoulders. He bent over and kissed her on both cheeks.

Her car disappeared into a welcoming curtain of white, leaving behind the lights of the house and the silhouette of the general standing in the opened doorway. Nina Ranevskaya took a deep breath. Swirling spirals of snow danced in the beam of her headlights. She was more terrified by Alexander Primikov's gentle words than the threats made from criminals she'd sentenced. The interior of the car was warm, the heater was going full blast, but she shivered uncontrollably.

She fumbled with her telephone and punched in Stroeva's private number. She couldn't get through, the storm was interfering with the reception. She glared out through the snow that was piling up on her windshield. The wipers were losing their struggle to keep up. She put down the phone and turned the defroster to maximum. She would try again when she got closer to the city.

The road was getting steeper and more slippery. The grade worsened. Nina Ranevskaya concentrated on the few feet the beams of her headlights could penetrate. With each gust of wind the road disappeared momentarily. The narrow mountain road swung around a rock outcropping. She didn't notice the darkened vehicle that blocked her way until it was too late. She slammed the brakes. Her car skidded to the left, smacking into a wall of stone, then veered sharply to the right and plunged over the edge. It hit something, then rolled over, slamming into tree after tree on its descent. The windows turned to spider webs. The door on the driver's side caved in. Twisted metal razored its way into the vehicle. There was a final jolt then the car came to rest.

A flow of blood warmed the side of Nina's face. There was a

metallic taste to the sanguine liquid on her lips. Outside, snow was falling from tree branches. A shaft of light bounced around the car. Someone was making his way down the snowy incline of woods.

"Help!" Her voice was little more than a whisper. She tried to see who was coming. A riveting pain from her ribs discouraged any further attempt to move. She was pinned.

A flashlight's beam lit up the interior of the car and rested on her bloodied mask. The pupils of her eyes were enlarged. They barely contracted when the light shone upon them. She was in shock, but very much alive.

"Help me, please." She gazed out through the shattered glass before her. All was black, except for the blinding beam from the flashlight. An unpleasant smell filled her nostrils, permeating the air around her. *The smell of gasoline!*

Whomp! The rush of air from the ignited gasoline reminded Nina of when she was a girl: it was the sound of her mother beating their carpet in the courtyard of the building where they lived. All around her red flames danced. The courtyard disappeared. Her mother now stood outside in the snow by the trees. Nina called to her, her voice exiting in a scream.

The phone in General Alexander Primikov's study rang. He had not gone to bed. Instead, he'd poured himself another cognac and sat, contemplatively, watching the fire. There was something peaceful in the syncopated rhythm of the flames.

The phone rang again. He reached over and picked up the receiver.

"The problem's been eliminated." Reassuring words, spoken by the one man the general trusted implicitly.

"Thank you, Major." Alexander Primikov replaced the receiver in its cradle and finished his drink.

CHAPTER NINE

THE White House considered Roger Glass a friend. He had contributed generously to President Thomas Benton's election campaign, served as advisor to the president on energy matters, and had entertained Benton and the First Lady at his Connecticut estate. Because of this, he'd been invited to the evening's reception and dinner for the president of Tajikistan. The country was sitting on top of vast oil reserves, perhaps as great as those in the Middle East, and Roger Glass wanted a shot at them. Benton's assistance had assured RGI's place at the table when the negotiations for drilling rights began in earnest.

Elizabeth Glass sat on one side of her husband. George Durmier, the finance minister of Belgium, sat on the other side. The table sparkled with white linen, crystal, sterling silver and celebrities. Around them buzzed dutiful young men and women in livery. America may have been a democracy, but not here and not tonight. Here, only the select were in attendance.

"It's a giant house of cards," Durmier droned on, warning Roger, and anyone at the table who'd listen, of the dangers of derivatives. "They're creating artificial relationships between disparate investment entities that simply don't exist in the real world."

Roger Glass wasn't listening. He had no interest in the complicated investment strategies that were turning world financial markets into gambling casinos. His only interest was who controlled the black flow that lubricated world industry. That, and the price of a barrel of crude were things he understood.

He glanced at his wife, who seemed to be enjoying the evening far more than he was. She was engaged in a conversation with Ryan Cassidy who sat to her left. For more than twenty years he had flamed the fantasies of young moviegoing women. Age and excess had now forced him to play more fatherly roles, when he could get them. Elizabeth Glass seemed unaware of the change.

"These so-called experts," Durmier went on, tapping Roger's arm to regain his attention, "are replacing sound economic principles with the flip of a coin. Fast returns. Easy money. No regard at all for the consequences."

Roger's eyes never left his wife. Even at fifty-two she was still striking. Roger wasn't blind to how men looked at her, how *that actor* looked at her. It wasn't jealousy Roger felt, merely the rights of ownership. What belonged to him, belonged to him, even if he no longer had use for it.

He hadn't married her for her looks. Elizabeth Gardner Whitingham brought with her a pedigree and connections to a world to which even his money couldn't buy entry. She was quality, old-line New England stock. Her grandfather had been governor of Massachusetts, her father a U.S. senator.

It was a marriage of convenience. Looking back, he wondered if it had been worth it. *Had he ever loved her?* He knew she had once loved him, but that was past. The truth was he had never loved anyone until Sidney.

"Excuse me, Mr. Glass," a secret service agent said, coming up to Roger's chair. Elizabeth and Ryan Cassidy paused in their conversation. "President Benton has asked if you'd join him for a few moments," the agent said.

Roger pushed his chair back and got up. A request from the president of the United States was a directive.

Roger and the agent exited the ballroom. They took the elevator up one floor, then proceeded down the thickly carpeted hallway and stopped before a closed door. The agent knocked.

"Come in." The voice was that of the president.

The agent opened the door, and stood aside to let Roger pass. He didn't follow, merely closed the door after Roger and took up his position in the hallway.

President Thomas Benton sat in a wing chair, smoking a cigar. He motioned for Roger to take the chair opposite him. A humidor sat on a low walnut table within reaching distance of the president.

"Help yourself," Benton offered.

"Doctor advised me to give it up," Roger replied.

"Nasty habit," the president agreed, "but one of the few vices left that won't get me in trouble with the opposition. I trust Elizabeth is enjoying the evening?"

"Very much so, Mr. President."

"And I assume you and President Rakhmonov had a profitable chat?" It was a gentle reminder. A favor had been done, a debt was owed.

"Time will tell, Mr. President."

Benton drew on his cigar then slowly released the smoke. "I have to get back to my guests, so I'll get to the point. How well do you know Alexander Primikov?"

"Well enough to call him General."

Benton laughed. "Frankly, I think he'd prefer the title of president."

"So I hear."

"Off the record, what do you think of the man?"

"I'm sure you know him better than I do, Mr. President."

"That's not what I asked."

"He's a tough negotiator, not a good loser and someone you wouldn't want as an enemy."

Benton put down his cigar. "Sounds like the two of you have a lot in common."

Roger Glass smiled. "Only I don't want to be president."

"Lucky for me." Benton leaned closer. "Between you and me, the United States doesn't look forward to a Primikov presidency." By *The United States*, Benton meant himself.

"From what I hear sir, it's not much of a possibility."

"That's what they said about Truman. Primikov's popularity is growing. Right now, the man's missing the power base and money to support his campaign. Stroeva's seen to the former. The latter, fortunately, doesn't seem to be on the horizon. But politics is a funny thing: one never knows. This country may yet have to deal with the likes of Alexander Primikov."

"I'm flattered you take me into your confidence, Mr. President, but I don't understand what all this has to do with me."

"Given the possibility of a Primikov presidency, I need to get a better feeling for the man. More precisely, will he advocate certain positions that might force us into another nuclear arms race?"

"I've met with him a few times, Mr. President. We've had certain business dealings together, but I don't see how that qualifies me —"

"I have all types of third-person reports on Primikov, but none of these supposed experts has sat across the table from him, negotiated with him, drunk vodka with him. You've done all that. That places you in a unique position."

"Perhaps, but —"

"In a few weeks Stroeva will be joining me at Camp David. Primikov will be accompanying him. I imagine Stroeva wants the general on a tight leash. I'd like you to join us."

"I'd be honored, but to what purpose?"

"I'd like you to spend time alone with Primikov, away from me and Stroeva. It will be a day or two of your time. "

Roger would have to rearrange his schedule, but the benefits for RGI could be incalculable.

"Naturally, if you want me there —"

"I'd view it as a personal favor."

"If you don't mind me asking, Mr. President, why me? I've had dealings with the man but I'm a businessman, not a politician."

"That's precisely why. Primikov knows you. He's already done business with you. I suspect he trusts you as much as he trusts anybody on this side of the Atlantic. That puts you far ahead of anyone on my team."

"And what is it, exactly, that you want me to say to him?"

"All in good time," the President said, crushing out his cigar. "My people will brief you in time for our meeting at Camp David. I appreciate your willingness to help in this matter," Benton said, knowing that Roger never would have turned him down. Not many people did.

"What was that all about?" Elizabeth Glass asked as Roger took his place at the table.

"Not now," Roger replied. The answer was unnecessarily curt.

There was venom in her eyes but she said nothing.

It hadn't been much of a marriage, certainly not the one she had dreamed of. Whatever love once existed, little remained. She had put up with his fanaticism to business, his constant traveling, even his infidelities, hoping that things would change. They never did. She considered a divorce. He wouldn't consent.

By now she didn't much care what he did, as long as he didn't embarrass her or her family. As for his indifference, she paid him back where she could. Spending his money was one way, accompanying him tonight was another. She was aware he hadn't wanted her to come along. It was precisely why she insisted on joining him.

To those sitting at his table, Roger Glass's personal stock had just skyrocketed. It was one thing to be invited to a state dinner; quite another to be summoned to a private tête-à-tête with the president of the United States.

Roger glanced at his gold Rolex. It was 10:00 P.M. He'd accomplished everything he'd come for. The festivities would continue for hours, but he no longer wanted to be here with his wife. What he wanted was Sidney.

"I've got to go," he said, turning to Elizabeth. The meeting with the president had given him the pretext he needed.

"In the middle of everything?" She didn't try to hide her displeasure.

Dutifully, she took the napkin off her lap and placed it on the table. Roger stopped her.

"I said *I have to go*. You stay and enjoy your new friend."

"Where are you going?"

"Presidential business, my dear," Roger replied. "I'll send the car back for you. See you at the hotel."

"When?"

Roger pushed his chair away from the table. "When I get there."

She was about to answer in kind when she realized she didn't give a damn.

"Try it again," Roger Glass demanded of the hotel's night manager. The man did as he was told and redialed the number to Sidney's room. Roger's tuxedo lacked the crispness it had exhibited at the start of the evening. His bowtie no longer fit snugly at his neck.

"Still no answer, Mr. Glass."

Roger made no attempt to hide his annoyance. He had wasted his time by coming. He'd intended to surprise her but she'd turned the tables on him. He'd called from the limousine, then again from the front desk when he arrived. He'd searched for her throughout the hotel. He had waited impatiently for her in the lobby. She was nowhere to be found.

"Give me a piece of paper and a pen," Roger ordered. The items were immediately provided. Roger scribbled a note, folded it in half, and handed it back. "See that Ms. Taylor gets this."

"Certainly, sir."

The hotel's heavy revolving glass door turned, depositing its occupants into the lobby. The smile on Sidney's face vanished. She let go of Ari's hand. Roger Glass stood by the reception desk. She hesitated, not certain of what to do. Her instincts told her to turn and run.

"What is it?" Ari asked.

It was too late to run, Roger had already spotted her and was heading towards them.

"My boss."

"Roger, what are you doing here?" Sidney managed to get out. She was amazed she could hear herself speak, her heart was beating so loudly.

"Waiting for you. Where have you been?"

"Out for dinner," Sidney replied.

He glanced from her to the man by her side.

The situation was a nightmare. Her world was about to collapse.

"A little late for dinner, isn't it?"

"I'm afraid that's my fault," Ari offered. "Ms. Taylor was kind enough to keep me company while I bored her with my work."

Roger turned from Sidney to the man standing alongside her.

"Roger, this is Ari Ben Lev, he's attending the conference. He's an exceptional scientist, from Israel, and his work is anything but boring."

"Ms. Taylor flatters me."

"I'm sure if Sidney thinks you're exceptional, then it must be true." Roger's words were laced with acidity.

"Ari, this is Roger Glass, my boss, chairman of RGI." It seemed obscene introducing her lovers to each other.

Ari extended his hand. Roger reluctantly shook hands with him. He had no intention of striking up a conversation. He released Ari's hand and turned back to Sidney.

"I need to speak with you, *now*, a matter of business."

"I thought you and your wife were having dinner at the White House," Sidney said. Ari was impressed, it wasn't often he was introduced to someone who dined with the president of the United States.

"I left there over an hour ago," Roger answered. "That's how long I've been waiting for you!"

"I'm sorry, Roger, but had you called and let me know I would have been here."

Sidney wasn't joking, Ari thought. Roger Glass obviously didn't think his employees were entitled to a private life.

"I should be going," Ari said, excusing himself. "Thanks again for the company, Sidney." He offered her his hand. It was strange not to kiss her goodnight. He would wait in his room for her call.

"Goodnight," Sidney replied awkwardly.

"Nice to meet you," Ari said, addressing Roger.

"My company does work in Israel, perhaps we'll meet again," Roger remarked.

"Perhaps," Ari said, though he doubted it. They didn't exactly travel in the same circles.

She waited for Ari to go, then Sidney turned to Roger.

"That was rude."

"Who is he?"

"I told you, a scientist."

"You two seemed very friendly."

She deflected with a show of annoyance. "Roger, I have a splitting headache and it's late. I have no time for this."

"Let's go to your room," he said, taking her elbow.

She pulled free. "Good night, Roger!"

Roger Glass was aware that the man behind the desk was looking at them.

"I'm tired and it's late," Sidney said. "There are things I need to talk to you about, but not tonight. I'll see you in New York."

He had handled things badly. He'd been annoyed, and now she was angry with him.

"You're sure that's what you want?" he asked.

"I'm sure," Sidney replied.

"Very well," he turned sharply and left her standing there, alone, in the lobby. She should have felt a sense of relief but she didn't. She wouldn't, until it was over between them.

CHAPTER TEN

THE corporate jet taxied onto the runway, then stopped, waiting its turn to take off. It sat rumbling like a bull ready to charge. Inside the main cabin Roger Glass sat comfortably in a plush leather seat, an empty glass by his side, leafing through the latest updates on current RGI projects. The events of the previous night were still bothering him.

Dietricht Boch, managing director of operations for RGI, sat facing his boss. On his lap lay a copy of the folder he'd just handed Glass. Dietricht's prematurely gray hair was cropped short. His wire-rimmed glasses accentuated the serious look on his face. The furrows above his brow were carved by his dedication to Roger and the company. It had already cost Dietricht two marriages. His loyalty had put him next in line to run RGI when Roger eventually relinquished control.

Dietricht sat quietly, speaking only when spoken to, aware that Roger was in a foul mood. Under such circumstances he had learned it was better not to volunteer more than was asked of him.

Elizabeth Glass sat reading a magazine, out of earshot of the two men whose day started early. From time to time she would stop reading to look at her husband. It wasn't a look of love. She was still fuming over the other night.

"We're cleared for takeoff," the captain's voice announced over the speaker. The attendant came by and took Roger's empty glass. She checked the other two passengers, then returned to her own seat. A few moments later the engines fired up. The noise and vibration steadily built. The Gulfstream thrust itself along the tarmac, eating up runway, then lifted into the air. When it reached 26,000 feet, it leveled off.

"Skies are clear and we have a tailwind of twelve knots behind us," the pilot announced. "We should be getting into La Guardia a bit early, Mr. Glass."

The attendant brought Roger a fresh drink and placed it on the table by his side. For most people it was early to be drinking. For Roger, it was never too early when he flew.

"Would you care for anything, Mr. Boch?" She smiled. She was pretty and most men would have noticed.

Boch barely acknowledged her. "Not now," he said, waiting for her to leave.

"What about Indonesia?" Roger asked, when they were alone, flipping back through the pages of the report he was reading.

"It's a time bomb waiting to go off."

"What's the government's position?" He tossed the stapled pages onto the table. "This tells me nothing!"

"It changes daily. At this point no one knows for certain."

"Then find out. We've got too much riding on this!"

"Our people are trying, but the new government's unreliable."

"What's your position?"

Boch didn't like having to guess but there was no way to avoid answering. "We'll be fine if the independence movement doesn't spread. East Timor set a bad example. It could definitely threaten our interests in the region."

"You think we should cash out? Take our profits and sell our holdings?"

Boch knew Glass better than that. Roger wasn't about to turn and run, it wasn't his style. He assumed it was another of his tests. *Roger enjoyed fucking with people's heads.*

"That's an option, of course." He wished he knew what Roger was really thinking. "But if we do, we'll be selling on the cheap. Personally, I think we should sit tight, ride it out for a while longer."

"If you're wrong it'll cost us millions," Roger said challengingly.

"It's a gamble either way," Dietricht parried. "A year from now we might regret not having invested more."

Roger Glass agreed but didn't say so; intimidation was still a powerful motivator. "It's your call, and your neck." He turned to the next item in the folder

"What's holding up the new test wells in Colombia?"

"Ortega. He has the ability to block RGI's drilling rights on Uwa lands." It was Indian property, but Ortega had been appointed by the government to protect their interests. Thankfully, he was more concerned with his own interests.

"He's still willing to cooperate," Dietricht said, "but that cooperation doesn't come cheap."

"I thought we already settled that problem?"

"We did, but Ortega wants a new deal."

"How much?"

"Another twenty-five thousand."

Roger was angry, but this was business. Emotions only clouded one's judgment.

"Give it to him," Roger ordered.

"What if he comes back again?"

"Remind him that greed can be a *fatal* flaw in a man."

Boch nodded and made a notation on his copy of the report. He was glad he wasn't an Uwa Indian, or for that matter Ortega. It wasn't unheard of for local troublemakers at RGI properties to mysteriously vanish.

One after the other, with decision-making speed and clarity, Roger Glass disposed of the various items in the folder. He came to the final status report: RGI's Middle East operations and the Al Wadi fields. He took a deep breath and exhaled his disgust upon reading the numbers.

"They blew up a section of pipeline," Dietricht explained. "We had to shut down for repairs."

"Fifty thousand barrels a day going noplace," Glass said.

"It's flowing again."

"For how long?" The question was rhetorical, the tone accusatory. Boch didn't respond. He was familiar with the players in the region. He'd spent a good part of his career in the Middle East negotiating contracts. He'd warned Roger but wasn't about to remind him of that fact.

"Who's responsible?" Roger asked.

"The Sword of God."

"Sons-of-bitches!"

He'd guessed wrong! The Sword of God had delivered on its threat. They'd warned him, but the exclusive right to drill on forty thousand Israeli acres near the Dead Sea had been too tempting to pass up. He had ignored the threat and Boch's counsel. The disruption at Al Wadi was the result.

There would be more trouble. Roger Glass understood that now. Still, he'd seen the geophysical and seismic reports. There was oil down there — he was sure of it. It was deep, would require a 30,000-foot Emsco drilling rig to reach it, but if he was right RGI would be sitting on a huge new find. Because of that, he also understood why the Arabs wanted to stop the exploration — Israeli oil could change the entire political picture of the region. *Not that he gave a shit.* If there was oil down there, he wanted it.

Oil was what mattered at the time he'd made the decision to sign with the Israelis. If he hadn't done it someone else would have. He couldn't bear the thought of others making money that was rightfully his. Now, however, he was beginning to question his decision, a self-doubt that would never be verbalized to Dietrich Boch.

"What are you doing to protect our interests?" Roger asked.

"We've tightened security at all our operations but it won't solve the problem."

"How much do they want?"

"You're talking about The Sword of God."

"Everybody has a price." He was prepared to be reasonable if they were.

Dietricht Boch shook his head. "If we were dealing with Rachman, I could probably work something out, but there's a power struggle going on within the organization. It's anyone's guess who will come out on top. If Jabal Hussein wins, the only thing he'll be satisfied with is the destruction of Israel."

"Great. That's just perfect!" Roger struggled to come up with an answer. "What do you suggest we do?"

"I know you don't like to hear this, but we can always sell the lease, stop drilling in Israel. Then again, if test wells continue to come up dry, there may not be a problem."

A smile spread across Roger's face. "You're a God-damn genius, you know that?"

Dietricht Boch hadn't the faintest idea what Roger was talking about,

"No matter what test results show," Roger instructed, "tell our people to continually report our disappointment with the findings. Start a rumor. Let it be known we're thinking of pulling up stakes and closing everything down. I want to see some real negativity out there."

Dietricht Boch understood. The man who'd built RGI into the largest independent energy resource company in the world still had what it took.

"We'll buy ourselves some time," Roger continued. "Until we know for certain what's down there and who comes out on top. If it's Rachman, you'll negotiate a price."

"What if it's Hussein?"

"We'll deal with him when we have to," Roger replied. He closed the folder and placed it on the table. "With any luck the Sword of God will descend on him."

Dietricht Boch nodded his understanding. In the meantime, he'd continue his dialogues with Bin Rab, the Sword of God's spokesperson, a man with expensive Western tastes.

"One more thing," Roger said. He lowered his voice. "I want you to check someone out for me."

"Who?"

"His name is Ari Ben Lev. He's an Israeli, some sort of scientist."

"Any connection to what we've been discussing?"

Roger shook his head. "No." He stole a quick glance at Elizabeth before continuing:

"He's attending the energy conference with Sidney. I want a report on him... on both of them."

CHAPTER ELEVEN

The conference ended. The attendees headed home to their jobs and families. Ari and Sidney stood in the airport saying goodbye, torn by the uncertainty of a future they both craved. He was heading back to Israel, she to New York. Both needed to end a chapter in their lives. He needed to speak with Hannah; Sidney dreaded the unpleasantness waiting for her in New York.

"Don't be worried," Ari said, kissing away the small furrows on an otherwise smooth forehead. "It's going to work out, I promise." He gave her hand a reassuring squeeze.

"I wish you didn't have to go," she said.

"It's all right," Ari assured. He kissed her lips, tasting the residue of salt from her earlier tears. "We love each other."

"Is that enough?" she asked.

"It's all that matters."

She wished she could believe him but her judgment in matters of the heart had proven far less reliable than her judgment in science. She withdrew a package from her bag, wrapped in white tissue paper and bound with a green satin ribbon.

"This is for you," she whispered.

"What is it?

"Open it and see."

He slid off the ribbon and unfolded the paper. Inside was a pale yellow cashmere scarf. A card sat on top.

"Here, give me that." She took the wrapping and shoved it into her bag, then draped the scarf around his neck while he read the card.

Something to keep you warm, when I can't.

Love, always. S.T.

"Do you like it?" she asked excitedly. "I saw you looking at it in the shop window of the hotel."

He put the card in his pocket and felt the softness of the wool. "It's absolutely beautiful. I don't know what to say."

She adjusted the scarf, tucking it under the collar of his coat. "A simple 'thank you Sidney, you're fantastic and I love you with all my heart' would do."

He put his arms around her and drew her tightly to him. "Thank you Sidney. I do love you with all my heart."

"You'd better, that scarf cost me a small fortune!"

He kissed her. She pressed against him, not wanting to let go. Right then, driven by love and impulse, Ari made his decision.

"Come with me, there's something I need to tell you." He took her hand and pulled her along.

"Where are you taking me?"

"Not far." He led her to a waiting area removed from the crowd and made her sit down.

"What in the world are you doing?"

"I have something important to tell you."

"You're going to miss your plane."

"There's time enough." He sat across from her and leaned close.

"What I tell you can't go any further, you have to promise me that." Though no one was near enough to hear what he said, Ari still spoke in hushed tones. His behavior was making Sidney uneasy.

"Ari, what's gotten into you?"

"First your word that you'll tell no one."

"You're getting me worried."

"Promise," Ari instructed.

"Okay, I promise."

His face took on a childlike excitement.

"I've done it."

"Done what?"

"Solved the problems that Kohl referred to that first night in the hotel bar."

"I don't have the faintest idea of what you're talking about."

"He said, the two stumbling blocks to making fuel cells economically viable were *size and cost*. He was right."

"Okay, so he's right."

A smile spread across Ari's face. "I've solved those problems. I've found the replacement for carbon fuels. A clean, cheap, virtually limitless supply of energy."

She couldn't help herself, she laughed. It was hardly the response he'd envisioned.

"I'm not joking with you," Ari said. "Fuel cells are going to power cars, planes, even light our homes."

"One day, you mean."

Ari shook his head. He reached across and took her hands in his own. "Now. I've already done it." He let her go and sat up straight, waiting for praise.

"You're not serious!"

"Absolutely."

"You've actually made it work?"

"On paper, yes. I'm still running protocols but if tests continue to prove —"

"My God! Ari, if you've really done what you say —"

"I have."

"You're talking about the greatest discovery since the birth of the industrial revolution," she said excitedly.

"Keep your voice down," Ari cautioned.

"And you're really not kidding?"

"No."

Sidney tried to wrap her mind around the possibilities of his discovery. They were limitless.

"You're talking about the end of fossil fuels."

"The end of using oil as a political weapon, the end of global warming and very possibly the end of poverty as we know it," Ari added.

"It'll mean billions in royalties!"

"If it were mine to sell."

"Of course it's yours to sell, you discovered it." He hesitated a moment before answering.

"It belongs to the Israeli government. I work for them."

"You work for Ergoden."

"It's kind of one-and-the-same." The things he had just told her could already send him to prison, there was no reason to hold back now.

"Since the birth of my country we've been dependent on foreign sources for energy. The research I do is part of an ongoing project to help us achieve self-sufficiency." She still didn't get it.

"Then you don't work for Ergoden?"

"Ergoden is the government," Ari confided. "The work I do for them is highly classified. I can go to jail for telling you what I did." He had just put his head on the block, his gift to her. It was his way of proving that he trusted her with his life. He thought she'd understand. He was mistaken.

"All this time you've been lying to me about who you are and what you do?"

"I had no choice —"

"Even now, until just a few minutes ago, you were going to get on the plane and not tell me."

"I've betrayed my country by telling you."

"You betrayed me," Sidney replied.

"No! I didn't tell you because I swore an oath to tell no one. If the people I work for knew of my breakthrough… If they knew that I told you before even notifying them —"

"Wait — are you saying they don't know?"

"Outside the two of us, no one knows. I was waiting until I finish my final tests."

The loudspeaker announced the first call for Ari's flight.

"If no one knows," Sidney reasoned with him, "then no one needs to know. There are people here who'd pay a fortune for your discovery."

It had never been about money for Ari. To buy things for David and Hannah, perhaps, but never for himself. He was first-and-foremost a scientist, not a businessman. From his perspective, the technology didn't really belong to anyone. It belonged to the world. The knowledge had always existed, waiting for the person who was clever enough to decipher it. That was what it had always been for him, a kind of game. A race to the finish line. Proof that he could do it.

"It's not mine to sell," Ari reminded her.

"It won't be if you say a word about this to your government. They'll take it away from you and you'll get nothing. Think about what it could mean to us. It's our big chance, don't throw it away!"

She was right about one thing: The moment he told them, he'd lose control of his discovery. As for his coming to America, they'd never let him leave. No way was he going to give up his work or turn it over to others to complete. *No way would they make him a prisoner.*

"I need time to think," Ari conceded.

"That's all I'm asking," Sidney replied.

There was a final call for Ari's flight.

"I've got to go," he said. Sidney took his hand, imploringly.

"Promise me you won't tell anyone until we've had time to talk this through."

It wouldn't be a difficult promise to keep; he knew there was still plenty of work to do before he had his proof.

"Okay. Only remember," Ari reminded her, "you made me the same promise."

Outside the waiting area, amidst the continual flow of people rushing through the terminal, a man with the face of a boxer stood by a pillar folding back the page of a paper he'd been pretending to read. He watched the two lovers, noting their animation. It was a pity, he thought, that he had never bothered to learn how to read lips.

CHAPTER TWELVE

THE small convoy rolled through the hilly terrain leaving a thick trail of dust in its wake. The narrow dirt road snaked through a valley of rock outcroppings and ascending hillsides. The sun was departing for the day. Long shadows stretched from the surrounding hills, offering the soldiers in the vehicles some relief from the oppressive heat.

Abud Rachman was returning from Kahlil, The Sword of God's most important training camp. Forty-five new recruits were in the process of being educated at the facility. The school's courses specialized in small arms, hand-to-hand, and explosives training. The most talented graduates were tapped to go further, the most dedicated were trained to give their lives to strike terror. For the time being, however, he'd ordered a stop to all suicide bombings. Jabal Hussein's protests had not moved him to change his position.

A jeep with a mounted 45mm machine gun took up the rear of the column. Rachman's command car, the third in the line of vehicles, was indistinguishable from the others, with the exception that the armor was thicker and capable of withstanding a conventional attack.

He'd never understood why American commanders painted stars on their vehicles. They might as well have painted targets. The only reason for such stupidity was arrogance and America's belief in its invulnerability. *They'd learned nothing from September 11.*

Rachman looked out at the reddish-brown hills. They were a far cry from the green fields of his youth and his father's farm. Both the fields and his father were long gone, along with his youth. He was tired of fighting holy wars. Too many people had died for too little. In all the years he'd fought, life hadn't improved for his people. He had inherited hatred and bitterness; he didn't want these things to be his children's legacy.

The car lurched. It felt like it hit a hole. The engine fired inconsistently.

"What is it?" Rachman asked.

The driver, too busy to answer, shifted into a lower gear and gave the engine more gas, attempting to keep it from dying. The engine crackled. The car bucked.

"With all this dust it's a wonder anything works," the driver grumbled.

Rachman had no time for a delay. If something was wrong with the vehicle, he wanted to know. There was important work waiting for him back at camp.

"We'll make it," the driver replied. The car bucked again.

Rachman sat back, apprehensively. He glanced out through the window by his side and returned to his thoughts.

Iradj Bin Rab was led to the two-room house that Jabal Hussein called home. The walls were made of sun-dried mud. The main room held a bed, a table, and a few chairs, but no other furniture. The small rug on the floor had just been used for evening prayers. Jabal was in the process of rolling it up.

"I didn't mean to disturb you," Bin Rab apologized.

"You're not." Jabal placed the rug on the bed. "Leave us!" he ordered, dismissing the soldier that accompanied Bin Rab.

"Sit down," Jabal instructed. "There are things we two need to discuss."

Iradj pulled out a chair and sat down at the table.

"What is it you wish to discuss with me?" Iradj asked, with some anxiety.

Jabal crossed the room and took the seat across from him. "All in good time."

As if on cue, an orderly entered, carrying a tray. He removed cups and saucers and placed them on the table before the men. Then he removed a sweetcake that sat on a wooden serving board and placed it in the center of the table along with a long-bladed knife.

"Allow me to show my hospitality," Jabal said. "First some refreshments, then business. Very civilized. Isn't that how you've been taught in the West?"

Iradj didn't respond. *Civilized* wasn't a term one readily associated with Jabal Hussein. He was well aware of what Jabal was capable of doing to those who displeased him.

With a nod from Jabal, the orderly lifted one of the pots and poured Jabal's tea. A few drops splashed onto the table.

"Idiot!" Jabal scolded, wiping away the liquid with a swipe of his hand, spreading the stain across the table.

The orderly backed off as if scalded, apologizing profusely. Iradj felt the man's fear. Very carefully, the orderly switched pots and poured coffee into Iradj's cup.

"I hear you prefer it to our tea," Jabal said.

"I enjoy both," Iradj answered.

"I don't," Jabal said. "But then, unlike you, I have no need to straddle two worlds. Milk?"

"Just sugar."

The orderly nervously proffered the dish.

Iradj took three sugar cubes. They made a small splash as he dropped them into his cup.

"Leave us," Jabal ordered.

The man was only too happy to comply. He exited the room, leaving Jabal and Bin Rab to themselves.

Jabal took a sip of his tea. "Drink," he said. He watched Bin Rab cautiously raise the cup to his lips. Jabal laughed. "It's hot, not poisoned."

Bin Rab took a sip. The coffee was excellent, strong, the way he liked it.

"If it's not to your liking," Jabal said, moving to call for his orderly. Iradj stopped him.

"It's excellent."

"Good." Jabal took another sip of his tea. "I'm pleased you approve."

Iradj put down his cup. "Why have you asked me here? What is it you want of me?"

Jabal picked up the large knife that sat alongside the cake and raised it like a saber.

"Trust!"

The blade came down with full force, slicing through the sweet-cake and cutting into the board. The two halves of the cake fell apart. Jabal impaled one piece with the tip of the knife and offered it to Iradj.

Iradj's eyes moved between Jabal Hussein and the cake. Carefully, he removed the cake from the blade.

Jabal smiled. "See? You took what I offered, not knowing if I'd move the knife. That's trust. You trusted me."

"I have no reason not too," Iradj said. Cautiously he brought the cake to his mouth.

"Ah, but can I say the same thing of you?" Jabal asked.

The cake stopped at Bin Rab's lips.

"I am asking if I can I count on you," Jabal said, the knife still in his hand.

Iradj was unsure where this was going but he was certain of one thing: If he answered wrong, he would never leave the room.

The rocket struck the third car in the convoy, lifting it into the air. It hung there a moment, defying gravity, floating on the ball of flames. Then it blew apart, sending shards of metal and glass in every direction.

The convoy screeched to a halt. Soldiers jumped from the vehicles firing their weapons at anything that moved and seeking cover. An officer in the lead car shouted orders, pointing at a dissipating trail of smoke that emanated from the western hillside.

"Over there!" He pointed to a rock outcropping. The sun behind the ridge made it difficult to see.

The machine gun mounted on the back of one of the jeeps opened fire. Bullets tore up the crest of the hillside where the rocket had come from. The jeep roared forward, its gun blazing. Men on the ground advanced, spreading out, firing, running up the hill, and seeking whatever shelter they could find on the way.

A second rocket whined. There was a deafening explosion and the driver of the jeep was blown into the air. The soldier manning the machine gun disappeared into a wall of black smoke. The jeep burst into flame and tumbled down the hill, engulfed in a ball of fire. It came to rest on its back, its wheels spinning like a wounded insect.

The soldiers ascending the hill slowed now, no longer so eager to leave their positions of safety. They fired indiscriminately. No one was anxious to become a martyr. They shot at shadows, inching their way closer to the man or men who controlled the hilltop.

By the time the first soldier reached the position from which the rockets were launched, their attacker was long gone.

The coffee remaining in Iradj Bin Rab's cup had grown cold; he had lost all interest in it. He was aware that Rachman and Jabal had grown apart, but until now he never quite understood how much. He was being asked to choose sides. Jabal demanded his loyalty, Rachman merely expected it.

Iradj understood that the ground beneath his feet was treacherous. *How could he commit to one when he didn't know who would come out on top?*

"No more games," Jabal said. "Can I count on you?"

The knock on the door gave Iradj a momentary reprieve.

"What is it!" Jabal barked, annoyed at being interrupted.

The man who entered was one of Jabal's aides. Upon seeing Iradj, he hesitated, then crossed the room and came directly over to Jabal. He bent close and whispered something that Bin Rab couldn't make out. Whatever the news, it was important.

"Apprise the others," Jabal said, "I'll be there shortly." The soldier snapped to attention, then departed as quickly as he came.

"I'm afraid our meeting will have to wait," Jabal said, pushing his chair away from the table.

"What's happened?"

"Rachman's dead."

The news rocked Iradj Bin Rab's well-ordered world.

"No!"

"I'm afraid it's so," Jabal replied, already on his feet. His face showed no emotion.

Iradj struggled to remain calm, thankful that he hadn't been quick to answer Jabal's demand. He got up, missed his footing but caught himself.

"And there can be no mistake?"

Jabal shook his head.

"How?"

"A rocket attack. His convoy was hit by an Israeli ground assault. His car took a direct hit."

"The assassins?"

"Escaped, but we'll find them."

It was unlike the Israelis to risk ground troops in what amounted to a suicide mission. Iradj didn't share that thought. With Abud's death, everything changed.

"What now?"

"I am assuming command. There must be no vacuum left by Abud's death," Jabal said.

Rachman's successor had just been appointed. It was no longer necessary for Iradj to choose between them. His future would now be decided by his ability to adapt, a talent already well tested.

"What can I do?" Iradj asked, showing his support for the new head of the Sword of God.

"You will prepare an appropriate statement condemning the Zionist State, holding them responsible for the consequences of their actions," Jabal ordered. "Nothing is to go out without my approval."

"I understand," Iradj replied.

"Good. Abud's death will be avenged. Israel will be awash in blood."

The door swung open. "That will not be necessary," Abud Rachman said, entering the room. "I could not help but overhear." There was not a mark on him, nor was he a ghost.

"Allah has been merciful!" Jabal said, attempting to recover his composure.

"Praise be to Allah," Bin Rab exclaimed.

Jabal embraced Abud Rachman like a lost brother. "We were informed you'd been killed."

"You were informed wrong. There was much confusion. A dispatch was sent reporting my death. I thought it best not to correct the mistake, seeing that whoever tried to kill me thought he'd achieved his objective."

"But your car? I was told no one could have —"

"I was not in it. Mechanical difficulties had forced me to switch vehicles."

"I will see to it that Israel is made to pay dearly for this!" Jabal exclaimed.

"You will do nothing yet," Rachman countered. "Not until we are certain who is behind the attack."

"We already know," Jabal began.

"Perhaps, but it is strange how the Israelis knew the road I'd be travelling, and which car was mine."

Iradj had thought the same but remained silent.

"If there is a traitor amongst us," Jabal replied, "I will find him and serve you his head."

"I am comforted by your concern," Rachman said. "With Allah's blessing we will catch the one who led the attack. When we do, he will lead us to the traitor."

Iradj doubted that Rachman's attacker, if he were found, would be found alive.

Rachman glanced from Jabal to Iradj. "But I apologize," he said, "I can see that I have disturbed your meeting."

CHAPTER THIRTEEN

Sheet music rested on a stand on the dining room table where Hannah was giving her lesson. The strains of Mozart's *Violin Concerto #1* filled the apartment. Ari sat in the living room, in an old overstuffed chair that had seen its better days but which he refused to part with despite Hannah's protests. It was his chair. Though the material was worn, the feathers beginning to work their way through the pillows, Ari considered it with the same sentimentality as one would a failing pet who'd been a faithful member of the family.

A book lay opened in his lap, the page he was reading lit by the floor lamp by his side. He'd just read the same paragraph for a third time and still had no idea what it said. Thoughts of his fuel cell and of Sidney, Hannah, and David competed for his attention.

He gave up pretending to read, put his head back and concentrated on the music that floated in from the dining room. The playing was lovely, the violin soft and soothing. He closed his eyes, allowing himself to be swept along.

The music paused. When it started again it was from the beginning. This time different fingers moved along different strings. Unsteady notes played by uncertain hands. What came out was hardly Mozart.

The music stopped. "You must feel the music," Hannah instructed. "Listen."

Once more Ari was lifted by the lightness of the notes.

Hannah was still a beautiful woman. Strands of gray showed in her hair and her skin wasn't tight like when she was young, but her eyes still shined brightly and her fingers still seduced the strings of her violin. She was the lover of his youth, the mother of his child, and it was ending. The last thing in the world he wanted to do was to hurt her, though he knew he would. Life was so unpredictable and so infinitely sad, he thought.

The lesson ended, both teacher and pupil were grateful. The boy packed up his instrument, bid Hannah Lev goodnight and headed out into the chilly night air. A few moments later she entered the living room and came over to where Ari was sitting. His book lay open in his lap, his head rested against the soft back of the chair, his eyes were closed. She bent over and kissed him on his forehead.

"Are you sleeping?"

Ari opened his eyes and looked up at her. "I was just thinking."

"What?"

"That it's best that Mozart's dead."

Hannah laughed. "Be nice."

"Doesn't he ever get better?"

"Not that I've noticed." She came around and lowered herself onto the arm of the chair. Ari slid his arm around her waist.

"You play so beautifully. Sometimes I forget how really talented you are."

"Were," she said. "If you're trying to flatter me, it's working," she gave him a kiss. Her lips lingered.

His hand found its way to her breast.

Hannah removed it. "Don't get any ideas. I've got to start dinner and David could come in." She started to get up but Ari restrained her.

"Wait."

The guilt he was feeling was suffocating. It pressed down upon him, constricting his chest and making it harder for him to breathe. They'd fallen in love seventeen years ago. He still loved her. Only passion, weathered by time and habit, had exited their marriage. Desire had metamorphosed into a pleasant cohabitation but it wasn't enough for him anymore. The mystery had faded, the blemishes appeared, and the divinity he'd created of Hannah vanished as her human qualities surfaced. The loss was inevitable but tragic nonetheless. Intellectually, he realized he would inevitably face the same process with Sidney, but his heart told him otherwise.

"I love you," he said, wishing it were enough for him. He brought her hand to his lips.

He hated himself for noticing the calluses on her fingertips created by years of pressure against the violin strings. The light that had erased passion had illuminated a plane beyond the carnal. There was no way he could tell her what he was feeling. It wasn't a choice between the lesser good but between two people whom he loved. His heart had already chosen.

"You seem so sad," Hannah remarked. "What's the matter?"

"Nothing, just thinking. When we were at the university you had such dreams of making your mark on the world. We both did."

"We were young," Hannah replied.

"Don't you ever regret giving it up?"

Had he forgotten she'd given up her career for him and for David? "If you mean choosing my family over my career, then no, I don't regret it."

"Everyone said you were going to be the next Perlman," Ari commented.

Hannah looked at him quizzically. *Why was he doing this?*

"What's the purpose of bringing this up now," she said, "it's over and done with."

"It doesn't have to be. You're still young. Lots of women your age restart their careers. " Hannah got up from the arm of the chair. He had meant to be encouraging, only he was making a mess of it.

"What in the world are you trying to tell me?"

Maybe it was time to get it all out into the open, Ari told himself. He never got the chance:

"Abba!" *Daddy*, his son called in Hebrew, running into the room with the toy Ari had brought back from Washington. "Look!"

"David," Hannah reprimanded, "your father and I were talking."

"But I have to show Daddy what I've done!" His eight-year-old enthusiasm couldn't be controlled. He climbed onto his father's lap and gave him the toy. "See!"

Ari examined it. It was a *brainteaser*, one of those impossible games that dared the holder to figure out the correct sequence of moves. When done correctly, all the multicolored squares formed the desired pattern. He'd tried to solve it himself without any luck. Somehow, David had figured out the right combination.

"Look at that." He held the puzzle up so Hannah could see.

David beamed.

"How did you do this?" Ari asked.

"I saw it inside my head."

Ari laughed. "When Einstein was asked how he discovered the Theory of Relativity, he gave practically the same answer."

Ari gave his son a big hug and a kiss. David giggled and squirmed in his father's arms.

"What do you think of our little genius?" Ari asked.

Hannah smiled. "I think dinner will be ready in ten minutes and both my geniuses had better wash up and get themselves to the table."

"You heard your mother," Ari said, giving the toy back to his son. He lifted David from his lap.

How can I leave him? Ari silently asked himself.

Jacob Barkan had canceled his last class of the day and left a simple note for his students tacked to the door: *Class Canceled*. From school he'd made his way across town to his other life.

Jacob couldn't understand the inaction of his superior. He had presented his conclusions, given him his recommendations. The man was a field-tested and hardened officer and yet he refused to act. For the last ten minutes Jacob had been sitting quietly, biding his time while the man across the desk from him continued to read the report. His name was Simon but most people in the agency called him Lazarus, a name given to him after the '73 war.

No matter how many times Jacob had seen the awful scar that ran from above Lazarus's left eye, down his cheek and through his upper lip, he still couldn't help but stare. It was a hideous thing. A remembrance from the Yom Kippur War, it was a gift from Lazarus's Syrian captors, who'd sliced his face like an onion. He had been left lying in a pool of his own blood while they argued whether to take him back for further questioning or to simply finish the job. None paid their prisoner much attention. He was thought to be beyond being a problem. They were wrong. *Rising from the dead*, Lazarus had killed them all.

He closed the folder containing the report and photographs that Barkan had given him. "What am I supposed to do with this?"

"I think the report speaks for itself. You've got my recommendation."

"And you expect me to bring him in on the strength of this?" He tossed the folder down on his desk.

"It's my belief —" Jacob began.

"I'm not interested in your beliefs! You make assumptions but you give me no proof."

"Assumptions are our business," Jacob said, defensively.

"Assumptions are guesses! Your job is to bring me facts."

"There are enough facts in there to bring him in."

"You want him brought in?"

"Yes."

"Then give me more than the revelation that the man's having an affair. If I brought people in for that, I'd have to arrest half the Knesset."

Jacob Barkan bristled. "I've worked damn hard getting close to the man. I want it in the record that I feel the man's a security risk and should be brought in."

"Your *feelings* are so noted."

"He's hiding something!"

"From his wife! That's all you've shown me so far." Lazarus took back the folder and flipped it open. He took out the photo of Sidney Taylor. "I certainly can't fault him his taste in women."

Jacob felt an impulse to defend Hannah. He let it pass. "And if his plan is to leave the country to be with her?"

Lazarus continued to examine the picture. "Still not a crime."

"It is if he intends to take his research with him."

"From all reports there's nothing to take."

"You can't be sure of that. The girl works in the energy business. He told me himself he'd made some sort of breakthrough. It's all in those pages. "

"What kind of breakthrough?"

Jacob hesitated. "I don't know, he wouldn't say."

"So it could be anything … or nothing?"

"I doubt it's nothing."

"Bring me the proof."

"By then it may be too late."

"If you think I'm bringing him in and risking the entire operation, you're out of your mind! You want him brought in, give me something concrete." He shut the cover of the folder.

There was nothing more Jacob Barkan could do. His gut told him Lazarus was making a mistake, but the call wasn't his to make. Jacob's only option was to push Ari harder. He liked him and had come to think of Ari as a friend. Betraying him wasn't easy. But he liked Hannah as well, and Ari had betrayed her. *What goes around comes around*, Jacob told himself reassuringly.

CHAPTER FOURTEEN

THE small shop was crammed to the rafters with used books of every kind. Shelves and tables overflowed with them. The back room was dedicated to older, more esoteric editions while the front room housed hardcover and paperback books of more current, mainstream writers. One could always find something of interest there.

Ari and Jacob frequented the bookstore regularly. They'd grab a quick falafel, Israel's answer to fast food, at one of the stalls in the Old City bazaar and head to the shop. Their shared love of 19th– and early 20th– century Russian literature was a part of the bond that had first brought them together. Czarist Russia had been a paradox that they never tired of discussing. Serfdom wasn't abolished until 1866, making it the last country in Europe to do so. The vast majority of the population was uneducated and bound to the land. And yet, a collection of some of the most brilliant minds in literature managed to push through that vast, frozen tundra: Tolstoy, Chekov, Dostoevski, Turgenev, Pushkin, the list went on.

Since returning from the States, Ari hadn't had time for lunches, let alone rummaging through bookstores. He had a mission: to prove his fuel cell worked. Everything else came second. Today had been no exception, only this time Jacob Barkan hadn't taken no for an answer.

Browsing leisurely amongst the tables piled high with books, Ari was glad he'd given in. He picked out a book with a faded red cover, *The Duel* by Anton Chekov, and began to leaf through the pages.

Jacob Barkan moved along the shelves, glancing through the rows of out-of-print literary works. A set of three leather-bound books caught his eye. He reached up and took them down. The set was old, but the spines were in perfect shape and the leather was still in excellent condition. He opened the top book and beneath a translucent, parchment-like sheet was a delicate etching of Beethoven. The set chronicled the lives of the great composers.

"Anything interesting?" Ari asked, putting the book in his hand back down on top of the pile.

"See for yourself."

Ari took the book from Jacob and glanced through it.

"What do you think?" Jacob asked.

"Hannah would love it."

"That's what I thought. I'm buying her the set," Jacob said.

Ari handed the book back to Jacob. The price had been marked on the inside cover. "No way, they're far too expensive."

"It's a gift."

"A rather extravagant one. I can't accept."

"They're not for you," Jacob reminded him. "Besides, I really want to get them for her."

It was so typical of Jacob. He was always buying them presents, always so generous and giving. Ari hated that he had paid him back with dishonesty. *It was only a matter of time before it all came out, anyway*. If Jacob was going to learn the truth, Ari preferred he heard it from him.

"Can I speak to you in confidence about something?" Ari asked.

"Of course," Jacob replied matter-of-factly, though his heart raced with anticipation.

"Is there someplace we can sit and talk?" Ari asked.

"There's a café farther down the street, we can grab a cup of coffee and talk there," Jacob said, taking Hannah's books to the register. He was moving closer to the proof that Lazarus required.

Hannah Lev never minded housework. Caring for her home, like caring for her family, was something that came natural to her. She picked up her son's shirt and spread it out flat on the ironing board straightening out the folds as best she could with her hand.

She enjoyed the back and forth repetitive motion of the iron, finding the process meditative. As the iron glided on a cloud of steam across the fabric, her mind straightened out the small wrinkles in her life. David was sniffling this morning when she sent him off to school. She was concerned he was coming down with something. She'd have to keep an eye on him.

She turned off the iron, carefully folded the small shirt she'd just finished, and placed it on top of the stack on the bed. Scooping the pile up in her arms, she carried it to David's room and put the things away.

When she returned she went to the dresser and checked her list. Only two more items remained to be done: food shopping and the cleaner.

She took the two pairs of pants from the chair where Ari had left them for her, checked the pockets, and placed the pants on the bed. Remembering that the coat he'd traveled in to America was soiled, she retrieved it from the closet.

She felt the bulge in the side pocket and removed Ari's gloves. As she did, a small, folded card tumbled to the floor. Hannah placed the gloves on the dresser, reached down and retrieved the card. She was about to place it with the gloves when curiosity got the better of her. She unfolded it and began to read. The handwriting was in English.

Something to keep you warm, when I can't.
Love, always. S. T.

Ari's coat slipped from her hand. Just ten words, but they struck a lethal blow. Her stomach spasmed. She felt physically sick. Her legs no longer could be counted on for support, nothing in her life could. She moved to the bed and sat down. She sat there for quite some time, rocking back and forth in the way Jews prayed for their dead.

* * *

It was lunchtime and almost all the tables in the café were occupied. Ari and Jacob managed to find a remote spot towards the back, away from the window that fronted the street. They sat leaning over the table, talking in muffled tones. The books that Jacob had bought for Hannah were wrapped in brown paper and tied with twine. The package sat on the floor alongside Ari's chair.

"Don't do this," Jacob implored, "you'll be throwing away everything you've worked for."

Ari had revealed few details about his discovery, but coupled with what Jacob already knew, it had been enough. As for the woman, he never mentioned her by name, only that she was an American scientist and that they were in love. It didn't matter, Jacob already knew far more than Ari imagined.

"What about Hannah?" Jacob asked.

Ari struggled to find the right words. "I'm not doing her a favor by living a lie."

It had been Jacob's job to make Ari his friend. He'd done it too well. His personal feelings now fought with his duty. He didn't want to destroy Ari, but he couldn't permit him to go.

"You're making the biggest mistake of your life," Jacob warned.

"I was hoping you'd understand."

"Understand what? I'd give everything I own for what you have." He meant it. Ari didn't reply.

"What about David?" Jacob asked.

That was the worst part. "What do you want me to do?"

"Stay."

"I can't," Ari said regretfully.

"So you'll see him when? On holidays? Summer vacations?"

"Why are you doing this?"

"To try to make you listen to reason."

"I've already thought it through."

"What makes you think this woman's not more interested in your discovery than in you?" Jacob asked, trying a different tack.

"She didn't even know it existed until recently."

"How can you be certain?"

"Because I am," Ari said defensively. "She'd never —."

"Never say never," Jacob cautioned. "People sometimes have a way of disappointing you."

"You don't know her."

"Are you sure you do?"

"Yes."

It was no use, he wasn't going to change Ari's mind. "When did you plan on breaking the news to Hannah?"

"Soon."

"And to leave Israel?"

"As soon as I can get things straightened out here."

Jacob was sorry for that answer, and for the consequences that came with it. His face telegraphed his disappointment.

"And that's final?"

"Yes."

There was nothing more Jacob could do to protect Ari from himself. He would speak with Lazarus first chance he got.

"Then I guess the only thing left for me to do is to wish you good luck," Jacob said.

Ari breathed a sigh of relief. "You have no idea how happy I am to hear that."

"We're friends," Jacob remarked. "What else can I do?"

"Can I ask a favor?" Ari said.

"Of course."

"Will you keep an eye on Hannah and David?"

"Of course."

Only you won't be going anyplace, Jacob thought. He checked the time. "We'd better get back." He picked up the bill.

"Let me get that," Ari said.

Jacob wouldn't permit it. He put the money down on the table. It wasn't twelve pieces of silver, but it would do.

* * *

They had just exited the café when Ari turned to go back.

"I forgot the books!" He'd left the package Jacob had bought for Hannah on the floor by their table.

The moment he disappeared inside, Jacob reached for his cell phone. He would demand to see Lazarus immediately. He punched in the number and waited. The supermarket across the street was teeming with activity. A car pulled up and the driver, an orthodox Jew, stepped out of the vehicle. His long black coat hung down to the ground. His beard was full, ringlets hung around his ears. He repositioned his hat and glanced furtively around as if looking for someone. His eyes stopped at Jacob. The two men stared momentarily at each other. Something about him bothered Jacob. Lazarus's line was ringing.

People exited the supermarket. A woman with a baby carriage filled with bags pushed through the opened doors. The little girl by her side held tightly to her mother's hand.

The orthodox Jew locked the door to his car and started to walk away. He glanced quickly, one more time, over at Jacob.

"Hello…?" Lazarus's voice echoed in the silence of the phone.

Jacob realized what troubled him about the man and the car: Today was a holiday. A minor one in the Jewish calendar, but a holiday nonetheless. No orthodox Jew would be driving on such a day!

"Hey you!" Jacob shouted, starting across the street.

Lazarus's voice faded as Jacob snapped the phone shut and shoved it in his pocket. The man in the long black coat stared momentarily at Jacob, then took off. Jacob reached for his gun.

"A bomb!" Jacob shouted, waving frantically for the woman to move. "Get away from that car!"

Time froze, then sped up. People were shouting, running in every direction. The street was chaos. The woman with the baby carriage grabbed her daughter. She scooped her up in her arms and ran. The carriage rolled towards the gutter.

Jacob never heard the explosion. Never saw its aftermath. The concussion threw him backwards into the air. Shards of metal and nails that had been packed with the explosives fanned out in every direction, seeking victims.

Ari was in the process of retrieving his package, his fingers reached for the string when the bomb went off. The windows of the café imploded. Fragments of glass and pieces of wood were turned into shrapnel. Tables were blown over. Chairs became projectiles. People were tossed like rag dolls. A black acrid smoke rolled like a breaking wave through the shattered window. In a matter of moments the café was transformed into a surrealistic nightmare.

Slowly, things came back into focus. Ari struggled to his feet. He looked around in horror. Broken glass glittered like diamonds amongst the mayhem. Faces and clothes were stained with blood. People were crying. Others were calling for those they couldn't find.

Ari's head ached and his heart pounded wildly. *He'd left Jacob outside!* He made his way through the debris that covered the café. When he reached the door he had to force it open. Glass fell and shattered before him.

Was he on the street or in hell? A smashed baby carriage lay on its side. The rising wail of sirens competed with the screaming cries for help. There was wreckage everywhere. Cars were burning. A woman, her face and clothes covered in blood, staggered by.

"Jacob!" Ari yelled. He could barely hear his own voice above the screams of the wounded.

A body lay in the street. Ari made his way over, bent down and cleared the smoldering debris away with his hands. He disregarded the burning of his flesh. He had found Jacob.

Blood mixed with the gray dust that covered everything. The skin on Jacob's leg was torn away exposing sinew and the white of bone.

Ari felt for a pulse. Jacob was unconscious but still alive. He took off his belt, and used it to fashion a tourniquet above Jacob's knee. He pulled it tight, slowing the loss of blood.

Ambulances were arriving, so were police. Medical personnel attempted to get to those who could still be saved.

"Hang in there," Ari said, not knowing if Jacob could hear him. There was no response.

"Over here, hurry!" Ari shouted to a man in a bloodstained white medical jacket. The medic rushed over.

"His name's Jacob Barkan," Ari explained, moving aside to let the medic get closer.

The physician checked the tourniquet and Jacob's vital signs. "Stretcher!" he shouted.

"Is he going to make it?" Ari asked.

The man didn't reply.

CHAPTER FIFTEEN

Davib heard the door and ran to greet his father. The sight of what stood in the doorway made him stop. His father's familiar face was scratched and puffed, the eyes were lifeless, and his clothes were soiled and stained with blood. His father's right hand was bandaged.

Ari entered and closed the door behind him. David backed away

"My God!" Hannah said, forgetting the welcome she'd rehearsed. David came to her. She instinctively put her arm around him.

"There was a terrorist attack at the market," Ari explained.

"Are you all right?" It was as much as she was capable of saying for the moment. Like David, she stood rooted to the spot.

Ari looked down at the blood on his clothes. "Most of it isn't mine."

"Your hand —"

"I burned it," he said. "The doctors insisted on the bandage. It's not that bad."

"Jacob's badly hurt," he added. He hadn't thought of the books until now. He had no idea of what had become of them, buried somewhere in the debris of the café he supposed. Going back for them had probably saved his life.

"Is Uncle Jacob going to be all right?" David asked, still holding on to his mother.

His answer was directed to Hannah. "He's lost a lot of blood and may lose his leg. He's in a coma. The hospital's supposed to call me if there's any change."

"What's a coma?" David asked, relaxing his hold on his mother.

"He's sleeping and can't wake up," Hannah answered.

"Is that bad?"

"It can be, now shush."

Ari moved from the hall into the living room. He stood taking in the simple things he'd taken for granted: the furniture, the pictures, a wall clock that once belonged to his mother. Everything, now, seemed more precious to him. It was wonderful to be alive and home.

"What did the doctors say?" Hannah asked.

"They're hopeful but they just don't know. He's lost a lot of blood." Ari took off his coat and was about to drape it on the back of the chair when Hannah stopped him. It was filthy and beyond saving. Dried blood was caked on the front and sleeves.

"Give it here." She held it away from herself, uncomfortable with touching the fabric, and carried it to the trash. David and Ari were left standing alone.

"Give daddy a hug," Ari said, bending down and holding out his arms.

David didn't move. His father's appearance frightened him.

"It's okay," Ari assured. He needed to be held as much as he need-ed to hold his son.

David approached slowly, frightened by the changes that battered him. Earlier it had been his mother's tears.

"David, go wash up for dinner," Hannah's voice commanded. She stood in the doorway watching them.

David alternated glances between his mother and father, not know-ing what to do.

"It's okay," Ari said, rising to his feet. "Do as your mother asks."

The boy ran off. Hannah stood staring at her husband. Earlier she'd wished him dead. It frightened her how close she'd come to having her wish granted.

What she had to tell him could wait. They would eat together as a family one last time, she would put David to bed, and then she would say what needed to be said.

Ari misinterpreted her silence. "I'm fine," he said.

"You'd better wash up as well."

"Sleep well," Ari said, tucking his son into his bed. That simple task meant more tonight than he ever could have imagined.

"Good night, Daddy."

"Good night," Ari replied, giving him a kiss. He got up from David's bed.

"I don't want Uncle Jacob to die."

"None of us do. Say a prayer for him."

"I will."

"Sleep well. I love you," Ari whispered, quietly stealing out of the room.

Hannah was waiting for him in the kitchen. She stood by the sink, washing the dishes.

"He's practically asleep," Ari said.

"We need to talk," Hannah replied, placing the last dish in the drain board.

"Can't it wait till morning? I can barely stand on my feet."

"No, it really can't."

Throughout dinner she hardly said two words to him. Whenever he asked her something, her answers were clipped. Now, when he couldn't keep his eyes open, she wanted to talk.

"What's so important that it can't wait?"

"This." She reached into the pocket of her apron and took out a folded piece of paper. She held it out to him.

"What is it?" Ari took the card from her. He opened it and read Sidney's words. His desire for sleep vanished. The ticking of his mother's clock competed with his heart.

"Where did you find this?"

"Does it matter?"

"It's not what you think," he said, fumbling for a lie that would make sense.

"I found it in the pocket of your coat and please don't insult me by denying it's yours."

He'd intended to tell her about Sidney, but not like this. Hannah stood waiting for him to say something, anything.

"I'm sorry," Ari said. "I never meant to hurt you."

"Go to hell."

He reached for her. She struck at him wildly.

"Stop," he said, trying to restrain her. She broke free and struck him again, hard across the face. In all the years they'd been married, neither of them had ever raised a hand to the other.

Ari stepped back reflexively, banging into the drainboard and sending the dishes crashing to the floor. The plates, which had been a wedding present from her parents, shattered. Ari bent down to collect the pieces.

"Leave them!" she shouted.

He picked up the one plate that hadn't broken and put it on the counter. A few moments ago he couldn't imagine anything worse than what he'd been through with Jacob. It was amazing how quickly things changed.

"Why?" Hannah asked.

"It just happened."

Her legs were unable to support her body. She leaned against the sink for support. "It doesn't *just happen!*"

"I wanted to tell you, I didn't know how."

"Was it me? Something I did?"

"No." He wanted to comfort her but didn't know how.

"Who is she?"

"An American I met at a conference."

"How long has it been going on?"

"Does it really matter?"

"How long?!"

"About a year," Ari confessed.

"You bastard!"

"Lower your voice, David will hear."

"Let him!"

"Hannah, please —"

"Do you love her?" She waited for what seemed an eternity for him to answer.

"Yes."

"Get out!" Hannah said.

"Hannah —"

"Now!" she shouted.

"Hannah, please —"

"This is no longer your home. You've made that choice."

"Where am I supposed to go at this hour?"

"Go to America, or to hell. I don't really care. Just go!"

"Hannah —"

"*Go!*" She picked up the dish Ari had saved. He thought she was going to throw it at him. Instead she threw it to the floor, smashing it to bits. He no longer attempted to reason with her. He went to what had been their bedroom and began to pack his belongings.

CHAPTER SIXTEEN

S HE was in her parents' house and for some reason Ari was there too, upstairs in her bedroom. He was calling to her. She wanted to go to him but Roger was holding her, preventing her from leaving. She struggled to break free. The more she struggled, the more violent Roger became. They were suddenly on the roof. Roger was dragging her towards the edge. It was straight down, and there was nothing for her to hold on to.

The ringing of the telephone pulled her out of the nightmare. Sidney untangled herself from the bedding and fumbled for the phone. Her hand located the receiver and lifted it from its perch.

"Hello?" She turned on the light.

"It's me," Ari said.

She was grateful to hear his voice, though she'd have preferred to have him beside her. She glanced over at the clock: *six forty-five*. It was afternoon in Israel. "I was just having the craziest dream —"

"I'm sorry I woke you."

"It's time to get up, anyway." She reached over and switched off the alarm.

"I needed to talk to you," Ari said.

"Is everything all right?" Sidney asked. Something was different, she could hear it in his voice.

"There was another bombing in Jerusalem."

"It was on the news last night," Sidney said.

"I was there," Ari said.

Any residue of sleep vanished. "Are you all right?"

"I'm fine, but Jacob wasn't so lucky."

He'd spoken so often about his friend that she felt she actually knew him. "I'm so sorry," she said, grateful it wasn't Ari. "Is he...?"

"He's alive, but barely. It's too early to know whether or not he'll make it."

"But you're okay?" she asked, to reassure herself.

"A few scratches, nothing serious."

"The bombing's only part of the reason I'm calling. Hannah knows about us."

"You told her!" Sidney said excitedly. *He'd finally done it.*

"I never got the chance to tell her. She found the card you wrote." The bubble burst. "What card?"

"The one with the scarf. I left it in the pocket of my coat."

"You what?"

"I know, it wasn't very smart of me."

"No, not smart at all." She was disappointed, but at least it was in the open now. They could move forward.

She got out of the bed and walked to the window. She wondered if he'd actually wanted to get caught. "Are you sorry she knows?"

"No. I'm glad that part's over, though I'd have preferred she hadn't learned about us this way."

That made two of them. Sidney cracked the blinds and peered out. A silhouette moved in one of the windows in the apartment building across from her.

"She asked me if I love you," Ari said. Sidney was afraid to ask his response.

"What did you tell her?"

"The truth, that I do."

The silhouette in the building across from hers stopped before the distant window and stared out in her direction. She quickly closed the blinds and came back to the bed.

"So what now?" Sidney asked, hoping he'd say he was coming to her.

"I've moved out. I'm living temporarily at a small resident hotel." He gave her the address and phone number. "For the time being, you can reach me here."

"What can I do?" Sidney asked.

"Remember the conversation we had in Washington, the one about Peterson? You can start making those calls now; I'll be needing a job."

"What about that *other* matter?" They never referred to his work directly over the phone.

"I'll give it two more months. If I can't get it finished by then, I'll take it with me."

He was bringing his discovery with him. They'd be together, and they'd be rich. Everything had worked out for the best. A couple of months more of waiting weren't much to ask for a lifetime of happiness. Except for that awful dream his call interrupted, the day had started out wonderfully.

Roger Glass's office was located on the uppermost floor of RGI's New York headquarters. The art and furniture were modern and extremely expensive. A massive desk of highly polished black granite stood in the center of the room. The couch and chairs surrounding it were of black leather. The carpet beneath was a rare Tabriz. Floor-to-ceiling windows provided a sweeping view of the tip of Manhattan, the river below, and New Jersey in the distance. The total statement was one of power and wealth. It was a monument to Roger's ego.

Roger turned to the last page of the report and continued reading. Dietricht Boch watched silently, anticipating the worst. He hated that he was the one who had to deliver the bad news. Roger would be out for blood and Dietricht didn't want it to be his.

Roger finished the investigator's report and put it down. "Seems that Nelson's done a thorough job." Glass's voice was controlled but Dietricht knew better. He was about to respond when the intercom saved him.

Roger depressed the intercom button on his desk. "What is it?"

"Ms. Taylor to see you, Mr. Glass."

"Have her wait." He got up from his desk and crossed to the wall of windows.

Dietricht remained sitting, following Roger with his eyes.

Roger stared out, considering his next move. It never paid to act in haste.

"That'll be all for now," he said, not bothering to turn away from the view. "Have Elise send her in."

Dietricht was happy to leave, though he'd have loved to be there when the shit hit the fan. Sidney had never been very nice to him. There was no reason he should feel any sympathy for her. *She's made her bed*, he told himself as he exited the office.

Roger looked out at the Statue of Liberty poised with her hand raised in the air, seemingly mocking him.

He'd trusted Sidney, and this was the way she'd repaid him!

The door to the office opened and Sidney entered. It was her first opportunity to meet with him since his return from Tajikistan, their first face-to-face since Washington. She wondered if he'd intentionally been avoiding her.

"Thanks for seeing me, Roger. How was your trip?"

"Close the door," he said, his back to her. She did as he asked.

"Roger, there's something I need to talk to you about."

"In a moment. Sit down," he said, not bothering to turn away from the window. His voice was ice.

Sidney took a seat in one of the leather chairs by his desk.

"Roger —"

"*In a moment,*" he said, turning away from the world he controlled.

There were half a dozen signs that should have warned her but she missed them all, focusing instead on the things she'd prepared to say to him. She crossed her legs, her foot rocked nervously.

She looked lovely, her skirt a soft gray, her sweater a pale blue cashmere. Pearl earrings graced delicate lobes. *She was a vision of innocence,* Roger thought as he approached her. Sidney's legs were crossed and he couldn't help noticing their shapeliness.

Aware of how he was looking at her, and not wanting to send him the wrong message, she rearranged her skirt.

"Roger, I need to sp —"

"You're looking quite beautiful today," he interrupted.

"Thank you, but —"

"Virginal, I'd say, if I didn't know better."

For the first time, Sidney became aware that something wasn't right.

"There's something I need to show you." He reached down and took hold of her wrist. "Come with me."

He led her to the window. Before them was a sweeping view of the tip of Manhattan. Below, the floors dropped away. He was well aware of her dislike of heights.

"Roger, you're making me uncomfortable."

He could feel her body tense. She tried to back away but his fingers held tightly around her wrist.

"One more minute."

Sidney Taylor glanced between him and the void before her. She felt lightheaded.

"What do you see?" he asked, making her look out at the water far below.

She was unable to speak.

"This building you're standing in is mine. I built it and I own it.

"See that ship down there?" A tanker was cutting a path through the waterway below heading for port. "I own that too."

"Roger," her body was trembling. She tried again to back away. He held her fast.

"That tanker cost me more than twenty million."

"Roger —"

"But I'd see it on the bottom of the ocean before I'd let anyone take it from me." He released her. She stumbled backwards, towards the safety of the center of the room. He followed.

"I forgot, you don't like heights do you?"

"You know I don't." She reached for the chair and lowered herself into it. Her skin was clammy. She closed her eyes to regain her equilibrium. When she reopened them he was standing by his desk.

"It'll pass," he said.

"Why did you do that?"

He picked up the report from his desk. "To let you know how deeply I feel about things that are mine." He dropped the report onto her lap. Sidney opened it. What was inside was devastating. She skimmed through the pages. It was all there, everything about Ari and herself. Thankfully, there was nothing about the true nature of Ari's work.

"You had me investigated!"

"Don't tell me I've lost your trust?" Roger mocked.

"You had no right!"

"I had every right! You lie and cheat and make a fool of me and I'm supposed to sit nicely and take it? I don't think so."

"I was going to tell you everything."

"Tell me what? That you've been *fucking* that Jew behind my back!"

She'd never seen this side of him. The pent up rage that spewed out of Roger frightened her. She got to her feet.

"I'm not going to sit here and listen to —"

"Sit down," Roger said.

"It's over," Sidney replied.

"It's over when I say it is." His voice was firm, his anger under control.

Sidney put the report on his desk. "People aren't things, Roger, you don't own them."

"You have no idea how wrong you are. Now sit down, we're not finished."

"Maybe you're not, but I am. I had hoped it wouldn't end like this. I'll clear out my things and —"

"You really think I'm just going to let you walk away? You ought to know me better than that, Sidney."

"You can't stop me." She turned to go.

"Don't you want to know what's going to happen to you and your thieving friend?"

She stopped and turned to face him.

"It seems that one of our accountants has discovered a sizeable sum of money missing from RGI's research fund, an account which you have discretionary authority over."

"There's no money missing!"

"The records tell a different story. The money went to an account in Switzerland under your boyfriend's name." It wasn't hard for Roger to construct the scenario. He'd used a variation of it to ruin a politician who'd challenged him.

"Do you know it's a crime, punishable by prison, for an Israeli citizen to have such an account? I'm afraid you're both in a good deal of trouble." He walked around his desk and sat down.

"It's not true, none of it is!"

"The truth is what I say it is. Now if you'll excuse me, I have to make a phone call to our financial people."

Roger picked up the phone. Sidney approached him. "Don't do this, Roger."

He ignored her and dialed his secretary. Sidney tried to stop him. He pushed her away.

"Elise, get me Sabatini in accounting. I want to speak with him about some irregularities I've discovered." He put down the receiver to wait for the call.

"If anyone's to blame, it's me," Sidney said. "Ari doesn't know anything about us."

"In that case, he and I should talk. It seems we have more than one shared interest."

"Roger, *please*, don't do this."

"Give me one good reason not to." He would have liked a reason to forgive her. As for Ari Ben Lev, the man had taken something that belonged to him. There'd be no forgiveness and no reprieve.

"What do you gain from destroying our lives?"

"Pleasure."

Sidney struggled with her conscience. Only hours ago there had been the promise of a new life. Now it wouldn't happen unless she was willing to barter the one thing that wasn't hers to give away.

The phone rang, Roger reached for it.

"What if I could offer you something that could bring you infinitely more satisfaction and money?"

Roger smiled; he was enjoying this. "I already have money." He picked up the receiver.

"That might change when Ari's invention comes to market."

What was she up to?

"I'll call you back," Roger said to Vincent Sabatini. He put the receiver back down.

"You've bought yourself two minutes," he said.

She had no choice; she was doing it to save Ari.

"He's discovered a new energy source, worth billions to whoever controls it."

Roger shook his head. "Your friend works for Ergoden. He's a mid-level researcher, I read his dossier. He's not capable —"

"Ergoden's a cover, a part of the Israeli government. They've been working for years on a top-secret project to achieve energy self-sufficiency. And Ari's not only capable, he's done it."

"I suppose he told you all this?"

"Yes."

"Then you're an even bigger fool than I've been." He reached for the phone.

"He's perfected the technology for a new type of fuel cell," Sidney pressed on.

"Fuel cells have been around for generations. They don't work," Roger countered.

"They do now."

He studied her; his hand moved away from the phone. "Supposing for a moment I actually believe you; what does it have to do with me?"

"He's leaving Israel and bringing his discovery with him to the States."

"His government would never let it out of the country," Roger said.

"They don't know about it. Only three people in the world do: Ari and I, and now you."

"And he'd give it to me? Why?"

"Not *give* it to you, you'll pay dearly for it."

"And why would I do that?"

"Because that way we all win. Ari brings his discovery to RGI for development, you don't hurt him, and he never learns about us."

"And the profits from this new technology?"

"We share them."

"What if I say no."

"Then you have the pleasure of ruining Ari's and my life, but you lose the greatest discovery of the century, and RGI is probably out of business within ten years."

The vicissitudes of fortune were hardly unique to those who made their living in oil exploration. This news, however, portended a bleak future for fossil fuels, the foundation of his empire. If what Sidney was telling him was true, whoever controlled Ari's discovery possessed unlimited power in every sense of the word. He couldn't afford not to take her seriously.

"And you're sure the technology works?" The earlier rancor in his voice had been replaced by greed.

"Every computer trial has come back positive. It works."

"Go on," Roger said.

Sidney told him everything, right down to the morning conversation she had with Ari and the bombing that had nearly taken his life.

"Okay," Roger said, "you've bought yourself time. If he brings his discovery here and it's what you say it is, we all get to live happily-ever-after. But if you're lying to me —"

"I'm not," Sidney assured.

"Then I wish you two every possible happiness."

"And you won't hurt him?"

"The man who's going to make me king? Hardly."

For a long time after Sidney had left his office, Roger Glass sat at his desk, thinking. He was a good poker player but he still preferred a sure thing to taking a chance. *It would have been so much simpler if Ben Lev and his discovery hadn't survived the bombing.* The thought clung to Roger like a nettle.

He knew human nature far better than Sidney Taylor. Ari and she could no more work for him than he could stand seeing them together. As for RGI's control of Ari's discovery, they were naïve to think the Israeli government wouldn't fight Ari's patent once they discovered what he'd done. Ben Lev worked for them. They'd challenge his ownership and win. Everything he'd worked for was at risk. Ari Ben Lev had taken Sidney from him and was threatening to take everything else. Wherever he turned, Jews were causing him trouble: Ari Ben Lev with Sidney, the oilfields of Al Wadi. Now they were threatening the very viability of oil and of RGI. He picked up the phone and buzzed his secretary.

"Tell Dietricht I want him in here, immediately."

CHAPTER SEVENTEEN

W HEN Ari appeared at the front door, Hannah's initial reaction was hope. It had been several days since she'd thrown him out, time enough for him to reflect on what he'd done. She thought he'd come to ask for forgiveness. She'd always told herself she'd never forgive him if he were unfaithful. Such intractable lines in the sand seemed stupid to her now and yet her pride wouldn't permit her to tell him as much. He'd hurt her beyond words, but if he asked, she was prepared to take him back. To take him back, but not to forgive him. Only, he didn't ask. He'd returned merely to take his belongings.

Ari looked at the framed photo on his dresser of the three of them at a happier time. Hanna's father had taken it shortly after the birth of their son. Hannah was in bed holding David and Ari was by her side. David with a mop of black hair and large dark eyes like Hannah's. Hannah looked radiant. It was a lifetime ago.

How nervous he'd been at the delivery, how totally helpless he'd felt, and how frightened he'd been for all of them when the crown of David's head began to show. He had prayed for a healthy child, nothing more. David was perfect. The birth had been a miracle that he'd been privileged to witness. Never had he felt so close to God. Never had he experienced such a sense of universal love. It was, indeed, a lifetime ago.

He put the photo on top of his clothes in the suitcase. There was no attempt at order within the bag. Personal items had been placed on top of one another as he happened upon them. Hannah would never have permitted such packing, but times were different.

"Where are you staying?" Hannah asked, standing in the doorway, watching him pack.

"I took a room at a hotel. I'll leave you the name and number before I go, but you can always reach me at work."

"How old is she?" It was a pointless question, one she'd promised herself not to ask.

He closed the suitcase, not answering.

"How old?" Hannah demanded.

"Thirty-two but age has nothing to do with it."

She was younger! Hannah had been certain of it.

"Next time call before you come," Hannah said, coldly. "The locks will be changed when you return. This is no longer your home."

Ari struggled to find words to comfort her. *I'm sorry. I didn't mean to hurt you.* Everything he thought of saying sounded hollow. He lifted the suitcase off the bed and carried it into the hallway, stopping before his son's room. David had refused to come out.

"Can I see him?" Ari asked his wife.

"You can try but he's not very happy with you right now."

Ari knocked softly. There was no response. He called his son's name then opened the door. David sat on the floor pretending to be reading. He refused to look up. Nearby, the toy that Ari had given him lay smashed and in pieces.

"David," Ari said softly, stepping into the room.

His son looked up but didn't move.

Ari walked over to him. As he got close, David sprung up and ran to his mother. She put her arm protectively around him. Ari looked over at her appealingly.

"Your father wants to speak with you."

David didn't reply.

"He's your father and he still loves you."

"I don't love him!"

She nudged her son forward. "Go on." She wasn't going to be the one to make David choose sides. Reluctantly, the boy approached his father.

"I'll be in the other room," Hannah said, leaving the two of them together.

"Come here, David." The boy came closer. Ari kneeled down so that his face was at the same height as his son's.

"I don't like you anymore," David said. "You hurt mommy."

"I didn't mean to."

"You made her cry."

"I know." He reached for his son. David's body stiffened to his touch. He kissed his son, gave him a hug and then released him.

"Don't go," David pleaded. Tears ran down his cheeks.

"I have to."

"Why?"

"You wouldn't understand," Ari told him. "I don't expect you to, yet."

"You don't want me anymore?"

Ari's heart broke. "Of course I do."

David threw his arms around his father's neck. "Don't go, Daddy. I'll be good."

"You are good. You're the best and smartest little boy in the world but I have to go."

"I won't be bad anymore, I promise."

The tears wet Ari's neck. He made his son look at him. "It's not you. You haven't done anything wrong. And it's not your mother. It's me."

"Don't you love us anymore?"

How could he answer such a question?

Sidney was troubled by fits of conscience. She had promised Roger things that weren't hers to give. The bar rose with each hour she delayed telling Ari. Emotionally, she was a mess. Tonight had been the worst. She couldn't get comfortable, tossing from side to side unable to fall asleep. When it came, it was never for very long. Her unconscious mind allowed no escape, even in dreams. It kept replaying the same nightmare: She had opened a door and stepped into nothingness. She was falling blindly through the dark. She tried to scream, to call for help, but no sound escaped her lips. It always ended the same: She awoke in a cold sweat, never knowing what awaited her at the end of her fall.

Sidney rolled over, opened her eyes and checked the glow of the clock: Four A.M. It had been less than twenty minutes since the last time she'd checked. Trying to sleep was a waste of time. Her hand reached out from beneath the covers, felt for the lamp, and turned it on. The glow hurt her eyes. She forced her body from beneath the covers and made her way down the hall to the bathroom.

She switched on the light. The glare off the white porcelain tiles proved no friendlier than the bedroom lamp. She turned on the water and allowed the sink to fill. The pipes screeched at being awakened so early. She bent over the sink, scooped up the cool water in her hands, and splashed it on her face. The early morning baptismal helped to clear her head. She needed to be completely lucid for the call she was about to make.

"You look like shit," she said, examining herself in the mirror.

The peach-colored silk of her pajama top was stained from errant drops of water. She dabbed at them with her towel and then patted her face dry. The skin below her eyes was darkened and puffed, her hair unkempt. Both would require some work before she made the call. It was silly, she knew, but she wanted to be at her best when she spoke with him. The preparation would give her time to rehearse what she needed to say. She opened the cabinet, selected the proper tools, and started to work.

When her transformation was complete, she glanced one final time in the mirror. Satisfied with the results, she turned off the light and went back to bed. She pulled her knees up against her chest, her back against the pillow. Being under the covers made her feel safe. She dialed Ari's number.

A phone somewhere in Israel was ringing. No one answered. She continued to let it ring. Someone on the other end picked it up.

"Shalom," Ari's voice greeted. She panicked.

"Shalom?"

"It's me," Sidney finally managed to get out.

"Sidney? God, it's good to hear your voice."

She hoped he'd still think so after they'd spoken.

"I was just leaving for the hospital," Ari said.

"Any change with Jacob?"

"He's still in a coma but the doctors say he's made it through the critical period."

Sidney pulled the covers up around her. "How are you making out?" she asked.

"Not great. My son doesn't want to speak to me."

She recalled the photo of the little boy with the big dark eyes that Ari had shown her. She was sorry to be the cause of their pain. "He'll come around," she assured.

"Maybe," Ari said without conviction. "What time is it over there?"

"Not quite five."

"Something wrong?"

"Quite the opposite." She exerted all of her will to sound up-beat. "I've got good news: My boss offered you a job!"

"A job?"

"You asked me to make some inquiries."

"You didn't waste any time. What did you tell him?"

"That you're absolutely brilliant and it would be the biggest mistake of his life if he didn't hire you. He's starting you at two hundred thousand."

Ari couldn't believe his ears. It was nearly triple what he was currently making.

"Plus a virtually unlimited R&D budget". She was selling like crazy.

"The real money, of course, will come in from your royalties. You'll be able to give your son everything: holidays in the States, the very best of schools —" Now he understood.

"You told your boss about my work!"

"You said you were bringing it with you. You'll need a home for it and money for continued research. Roger's offered to supply all that and more."

"You had no right without asking me first!"

"Ari, you're not making sense, a moment ago you were delighted with the news. Nothing's changed."

"A moment ago I had a choice, now I don't! If he knows, so will others."

"He won't say a word to anyone, he's promised."

"Like you did?"

"Think of your future, think of your son's future. It'd be foolish not to take his offer."

There was a long silence. She waited for him to say something… anything. "Ari, are you there?"

It was too late to turn back. "All right," Ari said, "tell him he's got a deal."

Thank God! He was agreeing to take Roger's offer. The worst was over. They were safe. She let go of the blanket.

"I love you more than you'll ever know," Sidney said.

He hoped so. He had just sold his soul for her.

CHAPTER EIGHTEEN

CAMP DAVID was established during World War II for President Franklin Delano Roosevelt. It was designed as a retreat from the pressures of state and the oppressive summer heat of Washington. From its mountaintop in the Catoctin State Park of Maryland, the ailing president was hopefully able to see the world a little clearer. Since then, it was used by every subsequent president, both as a quiet sanctuary and as an informal environment to host visiting foreign leaders.

The original small cabins had been replaced by larger, more luxurious ones. A swimming pool was added at one point, as was a skeet shooting and archery range, bowling alley, movie theater and heliport. President Kennedy had created riding paths, President Bush a gym and fitness center, and President Benton, a well-stocked trout pond where he could practice fly fishing.

A security fence encompassed the camp's uppermost 125 acres of rocky terrain, steep drops and wooded slopes. The original log gate that crossed the approach road had been replaced with a high metal structure that changed the look from rustic to maximum security. During Roosevelt's time, 130 marines guarded the grounds. After the war the number continued to decline until there were fewer than forty people, including maintenance personnel, on full-time duty. When the president was in residency the number went up to eighty. Such was the case as President Benton hosted the president of Russia and his party.

Roger Glass had arrived considerably later than he'd anticipated. Work had delayed his departure and caused him to run smack into a wall of bad weather. The fog had been impenetrable and his plane had been forced to land in Thurmont. From there he drove along Route 77 towards Hagerstown and the camp. The delay forced Roger to put off, until the following morning, discussing an extremely sensitive matter of his own with the general. They were to meet early, to take a walk before breakfast on one of the many nature paths in the surrounding woods.

"Rah-ger," Alexander Primikov said, pronouncing his name in such a way as to make it sound to Roger Glass that the general was speaking to him in Russian. "I presume there is a specific reason why you suggested we take this walk?" Except for the accent, the general's English was excellent.

"I have something to ask you, which I preferred to say out here." His breath was visible in the cold morning air.

"More questions? All last night at dinner you have come with questions. Friendly conversation to be sure," Primikov said with a smile. "Still, one might think I was applying for a job with your government, or your company."

"I'm sorry, General. I didn't mean to be so heavy-handed, but I had been asked to try to ascertain your position on certain issues."

"To what purpose, may I ask?"

"Well, it's hardly a secret that you intend to challenge Stroeva for the presidency."

"Competition is good, no?" the general said patronizingly.

"Not for everyone. Frankly, your ascendancy is not a pleasant prospect for certain people in my government."

Primikov couldn't help but laugh. "I would suspect not, but why are you telling me this? Certainly those who asked you to question me didn't instruct you to impart such truths?"

Roger Glass checked the path in both directions before he spoke. The wind made a whistling noise through the empty branches above their heads. They were alone amongst the forest of trees. There was no safe way to present his proposition to Primikov other than to say what he had come here to say.

"The questions I asked you yesterday were for certain people in my government. What I'm about to ask you now is for myself. It's a straightforward business proposal between the two of us, one that I trust will go no further should you turn me down."

"Am I to assume your president knows nothing about what you are to ask me?"

"If he did I might become a permanent guest of my government in a facility where the amenities won't be nearly as pleasant as those here."

The general's instincts signaled caution. "I'm listening."

"Do you mind if we keep walking," Roger suggested. He blew on his hands, wishing he'd taken his gloves. He was freezing, or perhaps it was what he had to say that chilled him. The two men continued down the path. With the leaves off the vegetation, anyone approaching them would easily be seen.

"If you turn down my offer," Roger began, "we've never had this talk."

"You and I have had dealings before, Roger —"

"Never like this." He shoved his hands deep into the pockets of his overcoat in an attempt to keep them warm. "I'm told you're in dire need of funds to take on Stroeva."

"I am not familiar with this word *dire*."

"That without those funds you don't have much of a chance to beat him."

Primikov bristled. He found the definition insulting, though Roger was of course right.

"Unlike America, the presidency of Russia is not *only* about money!"

"I meant no disrespect, General. But money, a lot of it, could help your cause, could it not?"

"All gardens require fertilizer."

Obviously, they had different views on money. Primikov thought it a necessary evil, Roger thought of it with reverence.

"I also understand that by appointing you Minister of Energy," Roger went on, "your president believes he's successfully neutered you politically, separating you from your supporters."

The general stopped. "Did you bring me here to insult me?"

"Quite the contrary, General. My intention is to help you become the next president of Russia."

Alexander Primikov didn't know what to make of Roger Glass.

Roger took his hands from his pocket and pulled the collar of his coat up around his neck. He was amazed that the general seemed unaffected by the bitter cold. The temperature was dropping fast. The air smelled like snow.

"Stroeva's made a huge mistake," Roger said, continuing on, "one that will cost him the election if you're willing to hear me out."

"Why would you want to help me when your government wishes me to lose?"

"Because sometimes, men like us see a bigger picture. And sometimes our personal interests aren't the same as those of our government's."

If the general turned him down, things could become uncomfortable for him, though not nearly as uncomfortable as if Ari's discovery found its way to market. *There was too much at stake not to take the chance.* He had thought it all through; there was no other way.

"You've got my attention," Alexander Primikov replied.

"I was told to find out if you would create any obstacles to U.S. peace efforts in the Middle East should you attain the presidency."

The general's feelings about Arabs and Jews were well known: *The Islamic Republics were responsible for Russia's current state of affairs. As for the Jews, they were troublemakers.* His dislike for them was the distillate of centuries of Russian anti-Semitism.

"There will never be peace in the Middle East. Even with all of

America's money you cannot buy it. Tell your president that if he and his government want to waste their time and resources pursuing such an elusive goal, he has nothing to fear from me. Whether or not Arabs and Jews go on killing each other is of little concern to me, provided Russian interests aren't jeopardized."

"But what if they were?" Roger asked. "What if Russia's future, as well as your own, was better served ensuring that the parties maintained their conflict? Would you actively further that end?"

"I don't like games. What are you saying?" Primikov demanded

"I can assure you this is no game. I'm only suggesting that sometimes one can benefit from turmoil. Russia's number-one source of hard currency is its oil exports. If the conflict in the Middle East worsened and a war engulfed the Arab oil states, the price of Russian oil would go through the roof."

"Hardly revelation."

"As the man in charge of that resource, your personal power would likewise skyrocket. Overnight, you could become the most powerful man in Russia."

"An interesting scenario but one I haven't given much thought to."

"Neither has Stroeva. But by appointing you Minister of Energy that's exactly the position he's placed you in."

"Perhaps, but without a war it's all meaningless conjecture."

"And with a war?" Roger let the question hang in the air.

"What does any of this have to do with the election?"

"Two million American dollars are waiting in a Swiss account for you to use as you see fit, for merely agreeing to listen to what I'm about to propose to you."

"Two million dollars just to listen to what you have to say?"

"It's that easy," Roger remarked. He took a piece of paper out of his pocket. "This is all you need to access the funds."

"Two million dollars is a lot of money just to get my attention."

"It's a down payment and a sign of my good faith. Fifteen million more will be deposited in that account if you agree to deliver on what I'm about to ask of you."

General Alexander Primikov, the would-be president of Russia, was well aware of what that kind of money could mean to his campaign.

"What exactly is it that you want from me?"

Roger spok the words in a whisper, barely audible above the wind. At first Primikov wasn't certain he'd heard them correctly.

"The delivery of a tactical nuclear weapon," Roger repeated.

Alexander Primikov stopped walking. He didn't know whether or not he was expected to laugh. Surely it was a joke, or worse, a trap.

"For a moment, Roger, I thought you were serious."

"I am."

"You want to buy a nuclear weapon?"

"Please keep your voice down, General. It's not the kind of thing one wants overheard."

"Either you're a fool or you think me one."

"On the contrary, I think of you as the next president of Russia."

"You're suggesting I start a war in the Middle East?"

Roger shook his head. "Neither you nor I will be starting it. A Palestinian fundamentalist group will do that. You merely supply the device. My part will be to see that it's delivered to the right people."

"You must be mad!" The general turned and started back along the path from which they'd come. Dried leaves and twigs crunched angrily under his feet. Roger hurried to catch up.

"General, please hear me out. A few minutes more of your time for two million dollars is not so much to ask."

Primikov turned to face him. "I don't know what kind of trick you're —"

"No trick." Roger handed the general the paper with the numbers of the Swiss bank account. "Israel will retaliate, the whole thing will be over quickly. The flow of oil will be disrupted for years. You'll be left in charge of a more powerful Russia." Roger's selling points came fast and furiously.

Primikov unfolded the paper and looked at the numbers. Two million dollars. *Expensive insurance,* he thought. His acceptance of the money assured Glass of his silence. He could hardly tell anyone of their discussion without implicating himself. He could, of course, give the money back.

Primikov refolded the paper and put it safely away. "Why would you take such risk?" he asked. "Or as I believe you Americans say, what's in it for you?"

"When you become president, my company would expect certain concessions, certain favorable oil leases."

"You would do this thing just for Russian oil?" Primikov asked in disbelief.

"It wouldn't only be the price of Russian oil that multiplies tenfold," Roger said. "My company's holdings are extensive."

"And what of your investments in the Middle East?"

"Oil in the ground is like money in the bank. The value of that oil, too, will rise."

Capitalism bewildered Primikov. Roger Glass already had more money then he could ever spend and yet he wanted more? Glass could have drawn a similar parallel to Primikov's desire for power.

"I'll never understand you capitalists and your American democracy." The words were meant as an insult. The intent didn't escape Roger Glass.

"That's because you confuse the two, General. Capitalism is one man at the top making decisions. Democracy impedes that natural order. There's no vote or majority rule in capitalism. I have thousands of people all over the world working for me. I have no interest in their opinions. Like any man of courage, I do what I think needs to be done."

"It would seem we're not so ideologically different after all," the general commented.

"Perhaps not. Only, no offense, General, we capitalists do a better job of it. In the end, people respond better to money than ideology."

"This leads us back to your offer," Primikov replied. "Even if I agreed to your proposal and assuming for a moment that I could supply such a device, how would you get it to the Middle East? We are not talking about a shipment of vodka."

"My company continually moves drilling equipment from one country to another. Right now a project in Israel requires a deep-well rig that will be leaving Russia from the port of Rostov in a few weeks."

"A few weeks is not much time to arrange for what you are asking."

"It's all the time we have. Either the device is aboard when the ship sails or there's no deal, no fifteen million, no rise in oil, and very likely no presidency."

"I don't like being pressured," Primikov said.

"Neither do I, but it's not of my making. We miss that window and we both lose."

"How do I know this isn't some sort of trap?"

"Because my neck's on the block right alongside yours."

It was true enough.

"Trust me Alexi," Roger said, using the friendlier diminutive. "Everything's been worked out. You take care of your end, and I'll take care of mine."

Roger thought of Dietricht. *If he did what was expected of him, all the pieces would fall neatly into place.*

"I'll need time to consider your offer," Primikov said.

It was beginning to snow. A flake landed on Roger's cheek and melted.

"Take all the time you need, only I'll need your answer before I leave today."

Alexander Primikov looked up at the sky that hung over the American Camp David. He opened his hand and let the thin flakes settle on his palm. They were small and not very beautiful. They melted almost immediately upon landing. It didn't compare to the snow they had in Russia.

CHAPTER NINETEEN

T HE nurse worked efficiently. She rolled Jacob carefully to one side to change his dressings, then moved him back, like a butcher packaging a roast. She sponge-washed him, then replaced the old hospital gown with a fresh one.

Ari came nearly every day, keeping a silent vigil. He sat watching the nurse. She was young and pretty. Jacob would have enjoyed the attention if he'd been able. He gave no sign of registering anything. For all visible purposes he was dead. It was only his heart that refused the diagnosis.

It was humiliating. Perhaps not for Jacob, who raised no objections, but for Ari himself. He found it embarrassing to be forced to bear witness. Jacob was like a baby, but babies were cute pink little things that moved their arms and legs. Ari couldn't help but wonder if Jacob was aware of what was happening. He hoped not. It was too horrible to think that his friend could be conscious and trapped in his own body. *It would have been kinder to let him bleed to death.*

The nurse reattached the tubes she'd previously disconnected. A few drops of urine spilled onto the new sheet from the catheter. She pretended not to notice.

"Mr. Barkan seems to be doing much better today," she remarked, filling the silence.

Was she kidding?

"I don't see any change," Ari said bitterly. The nurse stopped what she was doing to look at Ari.

"It's too early to give up hope. Your friend's come a long way. We've removed the respirator and he's breathing on his own, his pulse and vital signs are strong."

"How can anyone call this fine?"

"I know it's hard to see people you care about like this but I have a good feeling about Mr. Barkan. It hasn't been very long and he really is doing better." She deposited the soiled linens into a can and snapped down the lid.

There was a tap on the door.

"Am I disturbing you?" Hannah Lev said to the nurse, not noticing Ari until she entered the room.

"I'm finished here," the nurse replied, exiting the room and leaving husband and wife to face each another.

"Hello, Hannah." Ari said. He made no move to approach her.

She walked over to the bed and looked down at Jacob. His face was thinner than the last time she'd seen him. "Any change?"

"According to the nurse, he's improving."

She touched Jacob's arm, perhaps just to reassure herself that he was alive. His skin was warm and moist. He didn't move.

"I was just leaving," Ari said, reaching for his coat.

"Actually, I was hoping to find you here. I need to speak to you. I've hired a lawyer. You'll be receiving papers. I didn't want you to get them without hearing it first from me."

The news that she was filing for divorce was hardly surprising, and yet it pained him. He struggled to find the right words.

"Don't you have anything to say?"

"I'm sorry." Ari's response was so feeble that it would have been better for her had he said nothing.

"Was our marriage so terrible?" Hanna inquired.

"Of course not," Ari replied.

"Then why?"

It was a question that had no good answer.

"How's David?" he asked, changing the subject.

"As well as can be expected under the circumstances. He doesn't understand what's going on but he'll get through it."

"I never meant this to happen," Ari said. "I wish it hadn't."

What was he trying to tell her? "Are you asking to come home?"

"No, I know it's too late for that."

"Maybe not," Hannah said, impulsively. *It would be difficult but not impossible.*

"That wasn't what I meant." His attempt at kindness had only made things worse.

Hannah understood her mistake. This was the first time in their life together that she felt naked before him.

"I've got to go," she said, making her way to the door.

"I don't intend to cause any problems," he said. "Tell your lawyer I'll agree to whatever you want."

She turned. He could see the hatred in her eyes.

"I don't want anything from you! David's another matter, you owe him."

"I know."

"I've taken a job teaching music at the high school," Hannah told him.

"What about David? Who'll watch him?"

"You're unbelievable! Suddenly you worry about David?"

"That's not fair. I've always worried about him, you know that."

Perhaps she was being unfair, but she didn't care. "He's in school most of the day and my mother's offered to help when I need her."

"It's not necessary for you to work," Ari insisted. "There's going to be plenty of money."

"When has there ever been plenty of money?"

"I've accepted a job with an American company. It pays extremely well."

"You're moving to America!"

"I thought it would be better —"

"And you have the nerve to question me about *my* responsibilities to David!"

"I'm doing it for him."

"Don't you dare!" She was furious. "You're doing it for yourself. Just like you've always done. You're doing it to be with *her*!"

"Her name's Sidn —"

"I'm not interested in her name, I'm talking about our son! David needs a father."

"He has one."

"A lot of good it will do him if you're in America."

"I'm doing what I think is best," Ari replied.

"For whom?"

"Hannah, I don't want to fight with you. What do you want from me?" Ari asked.

She wanted him to stay, to ask for forgiveness, to come back home to her and David.

"You really are a bastard," she said, closing the door behind her as she left.

Nothing was working out as he'd hoped.

CHAPTER TWENTY

Nabil was twenty. He had tried to grow a beard to look older but the dark hairs grew slowly and unevenly, leaving patches of bare skin amid the wisps of dander. The effect was to make him look younger than his years.

He stood in the small open square of town, his back against the mud-brick wall, his hands bound before him. The wind whipped up funnels of yellow dust from the parched earth. The fine particles settled on his skin and dark lashes. They stung his eyes but he didn't dare close them.

On either side of him armed soldiers stood guard. More soldiers were massing in the square, converging from the narrow streets. He knew most of them. They had fought side-by-side and lied together about their conquests on and off the field. Many were no older than he was. In a normal world they'd be attending university. Here, in the village that served as base camp for the Sword of God, the world was anything but normal.

Nabil had sworn his allegiance. He had shown no cowardliness nor had he been disloyal. He had just had enough and simply wanted to go home. They had found him in the marketplace of the neighboring town and brought him back.

Soldiers continued to file into the square to view his disgrace. They had been ordered to do so.

What had influenced him to join up? It was hard to identify the single most important factor from the confluence of daily degradations and shattered dreams. Perhaps the absence of any kind of meaningful future and the poverty in which his family lived. Or maybe it had been the need to belong to something, to believe in anything. Then again, it might have been as simple as the gun they'd given him and the feeling of power it engendered when he pulled the trigger.

He was sorry now he hadn't followed in his father's footsteps as a bricklayer. Instead of building houses for his people, he had been the cause of the destruction of his family's home. The Israelis had bulldozed it, punishing his mother and father for his acts. Now he stood bound before his fellow soldiers guilty only of being homesick and tired of the killing. This public pillory was punishment enough. The beating, which he knew was to come, would be easier to bear than the humiliation he now experienced.

"Walk with me," Abud Rachman instructed Iradj Bin Rab. They passed through the doorway of his headquarters and stepped into the protective shadow of the building. The heat was oppressive. A slight breeze swept down the winding space between the buildings that served as a street.

"So Lebanon was less than successful?" Rachman asked.

"Unfortunately, yes."

Rachman smiled. He had expected as much. The Arab Alliance was an organization of Arab states and political entities that had never lived up to their name. The delegates couldn't agree on the most basic of issues. Syria, Libya, Iraq, as well as moderate Arab states such as Jordan and Egypt came together with representatives of Hamas, Islamic Jihad, and the Sword of God to find a common voice. If a common voice existed, no one had found it yet. The difficulty was not so much in objectives but in the varied methods of expression. Suicide bombing and the murder of civilians could not be sanctioned by nations that did business with the West. Nevertheless, Rachman had sent Bin Rab to keep tabs on the players.

Since the attempt on his life Rachman had become more careful, though he still walked the village openly and without a guard. It was important to be seen by his men. There was a delicate balance between being cautious and appearing frightened. Fear was weakness and weakness was an invitation to trouble. Bin Rab didn't worry about appearance. His only concern was his own safety. Walking in the open with Rachman made him a collateral target.

Three men hurried out of a building before them. Upon seeing Rachman they stiffened and snapped a salute. Rachman returned it. The men headed in the direction of the square.

"Have you spoken with Jabal?" Rachman asked.

"Briefly." Bin Rab wondered if Rachman knew about Jabal's meeting with the American. It was unlikely, and yet, Bin Rab found himself sweating.

"He questions my leadership and challenges my authority," Rachman remarked.

"He respects you."

Rachman looked at him skeptically. "He thinks that I no longer have the stomach to fight."

Bin Rab started to protest but Rachman cut him off.

"There's a reason Allah has created every animal with only one head," Rachman remarked.

Bin Rab and Rachman turned the corner onto a street so narrow it could accommodate only people. An old woman, dressed from head to toe in black, sat in an open doorway, a basket of peas in her lap. Her fingers mechanically removed the peas from their pods, throwing the empty shells into the street. A goat waited patiently to retrieve them. No sooner did they hit the ground than they were gone.

"Allah be with you, mother," Rachman greeted respectfully as they passed. She stopped her work long enough to return a toothless smile.

"The Sword of God is no different from any of God's animals," Rachman continued, "there can be but one head."

"No one questions your authority."

"Are you certain?"

Rings of sweat spread under Bin Rab's arms. He hesitated. "Surely my loyalty is not in question? I have no ambition other than to serve our cause."

"I am pleased to hear that. And what of Jabal's ambitions?"

It was dangerous ground upon which Iradj now tread. He could see the square before them. It stood openly bathed in sunlight. Soldiers were gathered everywhere. He felt the pressure to answer but didn't want to choose sides. The things he knew were dangerous, but not as dangerous as confessing to them.

"If Jabal has ambitions, he doesn't share them with me."

The soldiers moved aside as Rachman and Bin Rab entered the square. In front of them, a young man, little more than a boy, stood flanked by guards, his hands bound before him.

"There is some unfortunate business to be done," Rachman said turning to Bin Rab. "Let me leave you with a piece of advice: Choosing sides creates an enemy but not choosing can create two."

He left Bin Rab standing amidst the line of men and approached the youth who stood awaiting his punishment. The boy lowered his head, unable to look into Rachman's eyes. He had disappointed him.

Rachman put his hand on the young man's shoulder. The guards moved away. "You have let me down," Rachman said in a fatherly tone.

"I wanted to go home to see my parents. I am tired of the fighting." Nabil's voice cracked as he spoke.

"We are all tired and would all like to go home. But what do you think would happen if we abandoned our duties and turned our backs on those who depend upon us?"

Nabil fought against the impulse to cry, they were all watching him. He was wretched and totally humiliated. He would give his life for this man. "I'm sorry."

"I know," Rachman said. The boy could have been his son but then they were all his sons and he had an obligation to protect them by example. He turned and walked away, nodding to the officer in charge as he passed.

A stone was cast striking Nabil in the shoulder. His reaction was one of surprise rather than pain. Another rock crashed into the wall by his head, chipping away the sun-baked brick. More stones descended upon him; soldiers, friends and comrades were obliged to participate.

Nabil raised his bound hands, attempting to protect his face. A rock struck his forehead, opening a jagged gash. He became dizzy and disoriented. His knees gave way and the earth pulled him down. Still, the missiles came at him, like the stinging of bees, striking again and again. No longer did he try to ward them off. He saw his parents' house, the way it once stood, then only darkness.

CHAPTER TWENTY-ONE

DIETRICHT BOCH was tired beyond belief. In the last four days he hadn't slept more than a handful of hours, few of those in a bed. He'd flown from New York to Riyadh to Beirut to meet with people he hoped never to see again. He'd come close enough to death to feel its bony fingers reaching for him. Had he known before he'd left what he was heading into, he would have turned Glass down flat. Sitting safely in the back of Roger's limo, he was grateful he hadn't.

Roger had underestimated him. *It would cost him dearly for that mistake.* The thought made it easier for Dietrich to swallow the homecoming Roger had given him. There'd been no hero's welcome. No words of congratulations or pat on the back for a job well done. Not even the slightest show of concern for his safety or for what he'd been through. Even a simple *thank you* was too much, it seemed.

Dietricht glanced out at the slow-moving line of cars. The evening rush hour was long over but there was still an endless line of red tail-lights before him. Roger's behavior made it easy to justify having opened the sealed envelope, reading its contents, and making copies. He'd never questioned Glass's instructions before. This time, however, given the players, he wanted to know exactly what he was walking into. What was in the letter was so egregious, so unbelievable, that it had taken him time to figure out Roger's motives. It always came down to money.

The copy was safely put away for later use. Its existence was his insurance policy and a guarantee of becoming the company's next CEO. Armed with the knowledge of what the letter held, he had made the biggest financial bet of his life. He didn't consider it a gamble. He already knew the outcome. All he needed to do now was sit back and let events take their natural course. His hand stroked the soft leather seat. Its richness was comforting. He could get used to this.

It was the second time today he was making the trip from JFK to Manhattan. He'd arrived from Riyadh and gone directly to the office to make his report, only to have Roger insist he accompany him back to the airport. Roger was leaving on business. It didn't matter to Roger that Dietricht had just come from there, that he'd been traveling for fourteen hours and that he was dead tired. Dietricht looked out at the distant skyline of the city.

If all went as planned, the kingdom would have a new prince.

The limousine jerked, braking for the car ahead of them. The traffic was horrendous.

"What the hell are you doing?" Dietricht yelled. The man's constant stop and go was driving him nuts. He just wanted to get home, take a long hot shower, and sleep in his own bed. *Was that so much to ask?*

"There's an accident up ahead, Mr. Boch," the driver said apologetically.

"Well, get us out of here," Dietricht ordered.

"Yes, sir."

As the traffic began moving again, the driver saw his chance. He sped up and shot into the space to his right. The procedure advanced them a couple of feet, no more. The driver of the car he'd just cut off leaned angrily on his horn.

"It won't help getting us into an accident," Dietricht admonished.

"No, sir."

Dietricht sat back. So much in his life had changed over the last few days. When he'd landed in Beirut, everything had been arranged. If anyone asked, he was there because of the disturbances at Al Wadi. Damage to the pipeline had cost RGI time and money, no one could deny that.

The only difficulty had been finding an appropriate hotel room.

There was some sort of conference going on in the city and all the best rooms were taken. Eventually, like everything else in the Middle East, for a price a room had been found. Unfortunately, he never got to use it. A message was waiting for him at the front desk when he arrived. He made sure his bag was safely stored in his room, then came back downstairs and followed the instructions in the note.

He walked among the throngs of people who jammed the main shopping street. He was a good head taller than most of the shoppers. If anyone was gunning for him, he made the perfect target. He located the specified coffee bar, entered and took a seat at a table by the window. Anybody watching him had a wide-open view. So did he, but there was nothing to see, only the changing mass of humanity outside the window. The street was clogged with cars spewing pollution, like every other Middle East city he'd ever visited. He unfolded his newspaper and began to read, aware that he was undoubtedly being watched from the moment he'd left the hotel.

He finished his coffee and ordered a second cup. Twenty minutes had gone by. He wondered if he'd misread the note. Could there be two such places on the same street? The waiter returned, replacing the empty cup with a full one. The thick brown liquid was sweet. The Lebanese used too much sugar for his taste.

"Mind if I share the table?" a young man, no more than twenty, asked. His coloring and features were Arab but he dressed in American jeans and a T-shirt with an *I ♥ New York* logo emblazoned upon it. His English was almost without any accent, a product of MTV.

"I'm sorry," Dietrich said, "I'm waiting for someone."

"That would be me," the young man said with a smile.

Dietrich folded his newspaper and put it aside. "I was expecting someone older." He shouldn't have been, over fifty percent of the population in Lebanon was under twenty-five.

"It's my understanding you'd like to meet a friend of mine," the young man said.

"It depends on who your friend is."

The young man became serious, very serious. "Someone who can be quite dangerous if you're anything other than what you pretend to be."

"I pose no risk."

The man rested his arms on the table and leaned closer. "The risk is all yours Mr. Boch. Frankly, if I were you, I'd get up from this table and go back to America."

"A lot of money was paid to arrange this meeting."

"As you wish. Only, if you're really so anxious to die, why go through so much trouble? This is Beirut; for fifty American dollars, anyone would be happy to put a bullet in your head." His smile said he was enjoying himself.

"Let's just get on with this, shall we," Dietricht replied. He was nervous enough without some *kid* jerking his strings.

The smile faded, the young man was all business now. "See the store across the street, the one with the red sign over the door?"

Dietricht acknowledged that he did.

"Be standing in front, by the curb. A car will stop, the back door will swing open. They will take you to your meeting. If you hesitate or change your mind, the car will keep going. If you get in and are not what you say you are, they will most definitely kill you. Either way, we won't be seeing each other again."

With those words he left. Dietricht sat wondering what in God's name he was doing here. He wanted to leave and not look back, but he'd come this far and the stakes were too high to throw it all away. He paid the bill and did as he was told.

The wait couldn't possibly have been as long as it felt to Dietricht. He kept looking at every car that passed. None stopped. Passengers and drivers stared back at the tall, awkward-looking American with his pale white skin and close-cropped hair standing on the sidewalk in a business suit under the oppressive Lebanon sun.

It took all of Dietricht's reserves to remain standing there. Finally, a gray Renault stopped before him. The rear door opened, a man stepped out and Dietricht reluctantly got in. The man pressed back in next to Dietricht and the car sped off even before the door was fully closed.

Dietricht found himself uncomfortably sandwiched between two men. It was no luxury sedan and the fit in the backseat was tight. The men smelled of the same middle-eastern spices that permeated the restaurants. They drove in silence. When they entered Zahlah, a town not far from the Syrian boarder, the car turned down a street, wide enough for only one car at a time to get through. The car ahead of them suddenly stopped. The door of the Renault was flung open, and Dietricht found himself being propelled out of the car they'd been driving in and into the waiting vehicle. As they drove away, the Renault remained where it was, blocking traffic and preventing anyone from following them.

The man to his right took something out of his pocket and unfolded it. It was a hood, made of heavy, dark cloth. He attempted to put it over Dietricht's head but Dietricht resisted. For his trouble, he felt a sharp jab in his side. The second man had shoved the barrel of a gun into his ribs with enough force to drive the air from Boch's lungs. The message was clear; he stopped struggling. The hood was placed over his head and secured tightly, shutting out all light.

He felt himself panicking, imagining that he couldn't breathe. He wanted to remove the hood but knew it would be a mistake.

"Where are we going?" Dietricht demanded.

"Sit back, Mr. Boch," the man who had produced the hood said in English. "It's merely a precaution, for your protection as well as ours."

Confined in darkness, Dietricht found the words spoken in his own language somehow calming. He quieted down and gradually began to breathe normally. His side hurt. He wished they had prepared him for what had just transpired and for what was to come.

The sweat collected beneath the hood. He stunk of fear. The drive took forever. He lost track of time. He wasn't sure if where they were taking him was really far away or if they were simply driving in circles until he was hopelessly confused. If that was their aim they'd accomplished it.

The car stopped and the door opened. Still blindfolded, Dietricht was led inside a building. Arms supported him on both sides. His legs ached from the long trip.

"We're coming to steps," the man who spoke English said.

Dietricht felt for them with his foot. On the fourth step down he missed his footing. Strong arms prevented his fall. As they continued their descent, he was aware of a drop in temperature. Closing off one set of senses seemed to heighten his others.

He was led down a corridor. A door was opened and he was steered through. The hood was removed.

"Sit!" The man on his right instructed.

Dietricht lowered himself into a chair that had been prepared for him. His eyes adjusted to his surroundings. He was in a room with no windows. The men who brought him flanked his chair. A man he didn't know sat behind a table, staring at him. A gun lay on the table and the man's hand rested upon it. Iradj Bin Rab, the man who arranged the meeting, stood off to the side.

"Nice to see you again, Dietricht," Bin Rab said, as if they were meeting for a drink at a pub in Knightsbridge. He had been paid well to facilitate this meeting.

"Is all this necessary?" Dietricht asked.

"Such precautions, I'm afraid, are quite necessary."

Bin Rab's British accent seemed out of place.

"You've gone through a lot of trouble for this meeting," the man at the table said, "I suggest you make the most of it while you can."

It was the *while you can* that troubled Dietricht the most.

Bin Rab tried to mitigate the discomfort to a good client. "What he is saying is that you Americans have a charming way of getting directly to the point. Such directness would be apprec —"

Jabal cut him off. The reprimand was in Arabic but the tone was unmistakably sharp and Jabal's displeasure couldn't have been misinterpreted. He wanted no one speaking for him or interpreting his words.

The smile instantly disappeared from Bin Rab's face.

"Speak!" Jabal ordered.

Dietricht looked around pensively, his eyes moved to the two men who'd brought him. "What I bring is for your eyes only."

"Leave us!" Jabal commanded in Arabic. The guards did as they were told.

"May I?" Dietricht asked, reaching for the envelope in the inside pocked of his suit jacket. Jabal nodded, his hand closing around the gun.

Very slowly, Dietricht removed the envelope. He looked over at Bin Rab. The message he read in Bin Rab's eyes was that he was on his own.

"I come with an offer from the chairman of my company. A man who is most sympathetic to your cause." Dietricht got up and placed the envelope on the desk before Jabal, then retook his seat.

"What is it?" Jabal asked, picking it up.

"I wasn't told. I was merely instructed to deliver it to you and wait for your answer."

Jabal opened the envelope and took out the neatly folded pages. He studied them, pretending he understood what he held in his hands. He spoke passable English but could neither read nor write the language. He handed the pages to Bin Rab.

Bin Rab read their contents. Halfway through he stopped, shocked by what appeared there. He glanced at Dietricht for a confirming look, but the man's expression said nothing. He continued on. When he finished, he handed the pages back to Jabal, leaned close and translated their meaning into Arabic. *Roger Glass was offering him a tactical nuclear weapon.* Conditions were attached to the gift, everything was spelled out in the pages.

> *The man who brings you this envelope knows nothing of what it contains. It is better that it remains that way for the time being. A simple yes is all that is required. If you accept these terms, everything will be arranged.*

A simple yes and Jabal would be given the means to destroy his enemy. Dietricht knew the man would sell his soul for that opportunity. He understood it as well as Glass had.

Roger's driver had just passed the accident and traffic was beginning to speed up.

There would be no more trouble from The Sword of God at Al Wadi and RGI would be favored in all future negotiations once the new political structure in the region was established. These conditions, spelled out in Roger's letter, were nonsense. He knew Roger better than that. There was more to gain than oil flowing undisrupted at Al Wadi and a few oil contracts that would never materialize.

Once Jabal set off the bomb, either the Israelis would take him out or, given their war on terrorism, the American government would. No matter the outcome, the whole Middle East would be in chaos. Dietricht knew the price of oil would go through the roof. Prior knowledge of the event would be worth a fortune in the futures market. Glass would make billions. So would he, if he played his cards right.

The driver paid the bridge toll and headed for the downtown drive. Dietricht glanced out the car window. The lights of the city flickered in the black water of the East River. It looked so peaceful. He was exhausted. He closed his eyes and tried not to think about what was to come. He could, of course, still stop it by sending his copy of the letter to the proper authorities. It was a noble thought, but fleeting. He'd lose everything. He comforted himself with the knowledge that what was coming was not of his making. Then he focused on all the money, power, and privilege that would soon be his.

CHAPTER TWENTY-TWO

CAPTAIN OSTROVSKI read through the paperwork handed to him by Major Grigor Dourov. Dourov had the look of a man used to being in command. Ostrovski flipped through the pages. The correct stamps and signatures were all in place.

"Everything appears to be in order." He looked up from what he was reading, past the major to the two men standing outside his office. They stood by a rolling cart loaded with monitoring equipment. They belonged to Dourov. The taller of the two had just lit up a cigarette

"Put that out!" Ostrovski barked, his voice carrying into the hall-way. "There's no smoking anyplace within this facility."

The offender, a thin man with a gaunt pockmarked face, drew deeply on the cigarette before dropping and extinguishing it. He was Russian by birth, had served in the Ukraine until the USSR fell apart and the Ukraine became independent. Now, he, too, was independent. He slowly exhaled a stream of smoke through his lips.

"I apologize for my men, Captain," Dourov said. He lowered his voice as if sharing a confidence with a friend. "This is what we've been reduced to, the new Russian army: no respect and no discipline."

Ostrovski nodded, assuming all officers shared his distaste for the enlisted man. Like the major, he was not happy with the changes within the army. Fortunately, he wouldn't have to put up with it much longer. A few more years putting in his time and then he'd draw his pension. He glanced back at the papers before him, picked up his pen and scribbled his signature. He hated these surprise inspections. It was not that he had anything to hide, it was just that in these times of military cutbacks and worsening economic conditions, the bastards were looking for any opportunity to get rid of people. Even a minor infraction these days could cost one his job. He'd struggled to find some shared ground on which to ingratiate himself with the major.

He turned the clearance form towards the major to sign. "I went to the academy with a Pyotr Dourov, any relation?"

"Not that I'm aware of."

The papers authorized the major and his people to make a spot inspection of the warheads being stored in the underground facility. Major Grigor Dourov signed the form and handed it back. The rank of major was correct but his real name wasn't Dourov, it was Ivan Sobolev, and his orders didn't come from The Department of Nuclear Containment, but from General Alexander Primikov

Captain Ostrovski removed a copy of the signed document and handed it to the major. He pushed his chair away from the desk and got to his feet. The brass buttons of his uniform strained under recently added poundage. He picked up the cap that sat on his desk. "We were recently inspected. I thought everything was in order. Is there a problem?"

"That's what I'm here to find out," Dourov replied. "The last set of readings was confusing. Certain levels were troubling."

The response took Ostrovski by surprise. Trouble was the last thing he needed. He put his cap on and exited his office, heading for the elevator. Major Dourov and his men followed behind.

"Are you saying there may be leakage?" Ostrovski asked. The possibility frightened the hell out of him. A similar situation a few years ago affected half the people working at a sister facility. Behind him the metal wheels of the cart that Dourov's men were pushing rumbled along the concrete floor and echoed loudly down the hallway.

"I'm not implying anything at this point," Dourov replied over the noise. "My job is merely to collect and report the facts."

"But if there is leakage —" Ostrovski began.

"More than likely, equipment malfunction. Most of the hardware in the field should have been replaced long ago."

Ostrovski continued leading the way to the changing room. *The danger was obviously real. Why else send a team all the way from Moscow when they had capable people locally? If a warhead was leaking radiation, they were all in for it.* He took off his hat and wiped the sweat from his forehead.

Never during the entire history of the facility had there been a need to evacuate personnel. *It was just his luck it should happen on his watch!* He saw his pension going the way of Chernobyl.

Ostrovski stopped the major. "Are we talking of a lockdown?"

"It's premature to discuss that possibility."

"I've followed all procedures to the letter," Ostrovski said defensively. "If there's —"

"Why don't we just wait and see what the numbers show."

Dourov's assurances weren't comforting. Ostrovski continued on, more eager than ever to get the major and his men to where they needed to be. It was no longer his pension that concerned him. If there was a leak, he might not live long enough to enjoy his pension.

"If there's anything I can I do to help, Major —"

"You can keep everyone away from the area. At least until we know what we're facing."

"Of course." The request was one he intended to impose first on himself. He had no desire to be a hero. He'd leave them at the changing area and return at once to his office to wait it out.

They entered the elevator and descended into the gut of the beast. The four of them rode in silence. The elevator stopped with a bounce. It was not unexpected but Ostrovski thought it more pronounced than usual. The door opened and an armed guard snapped to attention. Ostrovski acknowledged him with a salute. The party exited, and continued down the corridor. The cart rolled noisily behind.

The stenciling on the door before them read *Restricted! Authorized Personnel Only*. A yellow light blinked overhead. Ostrovski pushed through. Sobolev, and his men followed. The metal cart banged with force into the door. Ostrovski turned sharply.

Sobolev shot his people a look of disapproval. "Careful with that equipment," he barked.

"Sorry," the taller man said, flashing Sobolev a grin that translated to *up yours*. The second man tried not to smile.

If it wasn't for the operation.... Sobolev didn't bother to finish the thought.

They'd been recruited for this assignment because of their special talents. If they pulled it off, it would be the last time he'd have to work with them. If they botched it, it would still be the last time.

Inside the changing area, gray metal lockers ran along one wall. Low wooden benches were fastened to the floor before them. Radiation suits and protective headgear hung from pegs on the wall. Large letters on the door at the far end of the room warned *No Entry Beyond This Point Without Protective Attire.*

The technicians began to suit up.

"Thank you for your help," Sobolev said, dismissing Ostrovski. "My men and I will take it from here."

"I'll see you in my office when you're finished," Ostrovski said, eager to leave.

"Very good."

"Try not to drop anything," Ostrovski said jokingly, it was his standard line. Nobody laughed.

The general had specifically selected the complex, which housed decommissioned warheads slated for disposal. It was far easier to penetrate than one that was actively hot.

The grounds were heavily guarded and well fortified. High, electrified fences surrounded the perimeter. Each morning soldiers cleared it of small animals that had been too curious. Occasionally, they encountered the warm carcass of a fox, but nothing more.

The facility was capable of withstanding almost any attack thrown at it. Cameras and motion detectors covered every inch of the grounds. An alarm system could be activated that would seal the core where the warheads were housed, making it virtually impenetrable until help arrived from the nearby military base.

The entire complex was designed to keep people out who didn't belong. What it wasn't designed for was to protect it against people who passed through those barriers with proper papers.

The warheads were inspected from time-to-time, and housed in what was essentially a hermetically sealed tomb: a dust-free, zero humidity vault of hardened steel, lined with lead, and built into a fortress of rock. There was no danger of accidental detonation, the arming mechanisms were kept elsewhere. Contamination was the greatest concern of those who worked here.

Still, the disappearance of a warhead, even a decommissioned one, couldn't hope to go unnoticed for very long. For that reason, Sobolev and his people were to remove only the canister that housed the weapons-grade plutonium and replace it with an identical-looking cylinder. The warhead, sans its payload, would then be put back in place.

As for the detonation mechanism, a device could be fashioned from one of several conventional sources that were all easily accessible. The building of a nuclear bomb was not all that difficult. Plans could be gotten off the Internet. It was the fissionable material, the HEU, the *Highly Enriched Uranium* that was impossible to come by. It was this that General Alexander Primikov had sent Sobolev to get.

If they were successful, the theft wouldn't be noticed until the fissionable material was well out of Russia and all traces of its removal erased. The Russian government, not wanting to panic the public and the U.S. military establishment, would investigate quietly. By then it would be too late.

As the three men entered the vault, Sobolev checked the time. Nine minutes had elapsed. So far, everything had gone as planned. He'd allowed forty minutes for the entire operation, the time of a typical inspection.

The shorter of the two technicians went over to the control panel and punched in the required sequence. The panel was identical to the one he'd trained on. A shiny steel door on the wall retracted and a conveyance mechanically rolled out like a slab in a mortuary freezer. Instead of a cadaver, an object capable of unbelievable destruction came to rest before them.

The second technician approached the gurney. He looked down at the warhead and blew air through his lips.

"Nice boy," he said, patting the warhead as if it were a dog to be calmed.

"Get on with it," Sobolev ordered.

"Easy does it, *General*. I'm not in your fuck'n army anymore. From here on I'm the one running the show."

Sobolev was seething but held his temper in check. He needed the man.

The rolling cart with the equipment was brought alongside the device and the two men began earning their money. Tools, milled to perfection and crafted for this singular job, moved in expert hands. The technicians were like skilled surgeons performing a delicate operation.

The casing was methodically opened, the canister holding the plutonium carefully detached.

The technician with the pock-scarred face removed it, cradling it in his arms. Catching Sobolev's eye, he began rocking the device in his arms like a newborn. "Care to slap its bottom, General?"

"Just get on with it," Sobolev ordered. There was no place in his world for such insubordination. He checked the time: eighteen more minutes had gone by. Thirteen to go. They were already running behind.

The shorter technician opened the large monitoring device sitting on the cart and removed the dummy canister hidden inside. He changed places with his partner and the canisters were switched. Tools whirled, minutes passed and everything was returned to its proper place. When they were done, the control panel was reactivated and the conveyor holding the warhead rolled back into the wall. The steel door reset itself.

Sobolev checked the time. The first part of the operation had gone off without incident. He looked over at the technicians. The troublesome tall one gave him a wink.

"No leakage?" Captain Ostrovski said with relief, repeating what the major had just told him.

"Equipment malfunctions, as I suspected."

Ostrovski looked like a man whose death sentence had just been commuted. He was prepared to celebrate.

"Will you be staying over, Major? Can I offer you —"

"Unfortunately not. My men and I will be leaving immediately, we have a long trip ahead of us."

"Perhaps some other time?"

"I'll look forward to that, Captain," Sobolev said, picking up the bayonet lying on the captain's desk. It was an unusual curiosity. Sobolev read the inscription on the blade, then ran his finger along the edge.

"Be careful, Major, it's quite sharp. It was my father's, a gift from the men in his command."

"A lovely weapon." With a dexterity that took Ostrovski by surprise, the major spun the bayonet between his fingers, then placed it back down where he'd found it.

"Thank you for your cooperation, Captain," Sobolev said.

"I trust it will be noted in your report to Moscow?"

"You may count on it."

The two officers shook hands, and Sobolev started to go.

"Major," Ostrovski called after him, stopping him before he made it to the door. "Not so fast."

Sobolev turned to face him.

Ostrovski moved the bayonet aside and picked up a clipboard. "You've forgotten to sign."

"Of course," Sobolev said. He turned to his men who'd been waiting with their cart of instruments by Ostrovski's door.

"What are you two waiting for? Load up and wait for me in the truck," he ordered. "I'll be there shortly."

Sobolev approached Ostrovski. He reached out and took the clipboard.

"There are procedures that need to be followed, even in the *new* Russian army," Ostrovski said with a chuckle.

The major began to scribble his name on the clearance form. His mind was on the nuclear device that was on its way out to the truck. That momentary breach of focus nearly cost him the operation. He had started to sign his real name, caught himself, and turned the initial stroke into a "G." He signed *Major Grigor Dourov* and handed back the clipboard.

CHAPTER TWENTY-THREE

LARGE spotlights lit up the dock and the freighter tied to it. People moved about the deck, making certain the cargo was secure. Others worked down below, on the pier. The last of the crates were being hauled aboard to be placed into the hold.

The Port of Rostov, like ports in most cities, was not located in a very good part of town. The buildings were rundown, crime was high and the people who lived and worked there were used to playing rough. From here, ships sailed through the Sea of Azov into the Black Sea, through the Bosporus and the Dardanelles to the Mediterranean and finally out to the rest of the world.

Major Ivan Sobolev smoked a cigarette as he stood by the truck. The crate he was particularly interested in was in the process of being lifted from the dock by the crane operator. The particulars on the crate read, *Emsco Drilling Rig, Hydraulics-2. Destination: Port of Haifa, Israel.* It looked no different from the thirty-odd crates of varying sizes that were already aboard the ship and stamped with RGI lettering. Large sections of the steel framework for the rig had already been secured fast to the freighter's deck.

A man on the ship's deck spoke through his walkie-talkie cautioning the crane operator to slow it down. He waved his free hand furiously but the operator had turned away to take a swig from the flask he kept to insulate himself against the cold sea air.

"Look out!" the man on the ship shouted into the transmitter.

The warning came too late. The crate, suspended in its rope web, slammed against the side of the ship. There was a hollow ring of metal from the ship's hull. People below scattered. Sobolev cringed. *Had he come all this way only to lose it like this?*

The crate jerked, then swung out and back again, into the side of the ship. The ropes strained under the pressure, but held.

"You trying to kill someone?" the man on deck shouted into his walkie-talkie.

The crate dangled in the air. The crane operator struggled to get his cargo back under control. The swinging gradually diminished. The sound of the mechanical winch was heard again and the precious cargo continued its ascent.

Inside the crate, cushioned within a hydraulic cylinder lined with lead, was a canister that contained enough fissionable material to take out the Port of Rostov and a good deal more of the city.

Sobolev watched the crate disappear into the hold. He heaved a sigh of relief. His job was almost done. He had accomplished what the general had sent him to do, the rest was now up to others. He flicked his cigarette away, opened the driver's side door of the truck and climbed in. He reached for the key in the ignition and started the engine. Then he depressed the clutch, put the truck into gear and drove out of the gate into the darkened streets. The road was cobbled and bumpy.

"A drink to our success, General, I mean Major." The lanky technician sat in the front passenger seat. One hand rested against the frame of the window, the other held the bottle of vodka he'd been drinking from. He extended it to Sobolev as a peace offering.

Sobolev declined.

"Come on, Major, let bygones be bygones, we both got what we wanted."

Again Sobolev declined. He was choosy with whom he drank.

"Suit yourself." He returned the bottle to his own lips.

"Give it here!" A hand reached out from the back seat to claim the bottle.

"Watch it! You nearly spilled it," the technician in the front seat chided, grudgingly relinquishing the bottle.

"The only place I'm going to spill it is down my throat." He brought the bottle to his lips and drank deeply. Air bubbles replaced the clear liquid in the bottle.

"Easy, it's not all for you!" The pockmarked technician reached behind him and snatched the bottle back.

"Don't worry, there's going to be plenty more where that came from. Twenty thousand American dollars buys a lot of vodka." He leaned forward and slapped Sobolev on the shoulder. "Not bad for a day's work!" He reclaimed the bottle.

"Here's to capitalism!" he said, bringing the bottle to his mouth.

They disgusted him. These were not men of principle. They had no feeling for Russia. It made what he had to do that much easier. Major Ivan Sobolev reached under his seat. His hand made contact with the gun. The truck rolled with the movement.

"Steady, Major," the man in the back seat admonished, "we're the ones doing the drinking."

Both men laughed.

The major brought the gun up, put it to the head of the man beside him and pulled the trigger. Blood and soft tissue splattered across the side window. The glass became a spider's web where the bullet passed through.

The man in the back recoiled instinctively. Sobolev didn't hesitate. He turned and fired a second time. The man's head jerked back as if kicked by a horse. The bullet entered his eye and exploded through the back of his head. The bottle fell from his hand, the vodka splashed out onto the floor. Two potential liabilities had been removed.

The stench of alcohol filled the truck. Sobolev found the odor offensive. He placed the gun back under his seat and cracked his window slightly to get rid of the smell. The truck and the bodies would be disposed of along the way.

CHAPTER TWENTY-FOUR

THE building directly behind the mosque hadn't been used in years for anything but storage. The exterior was in need of a facelift. Inside it was worse. Paint was worn and peeling, water had leaked in causing the plaster to blister and crumble. The plumbing was undependable and the wiring unsafe. No one in his right mind would want to lease it. But that was exactly what World Teachings, a fundamentalist Islamic charity, had done. Their offer to rent the place and pay for the necessary improvements had been far too generous for the elders to pass up.

The deal was struck, and the mosque received three-months' rent in advance. The work of renovation began immediately. A truckload of broken furniture and a mountain of papers stored in cardboard cartons had to move out and find a new home. Locks were changed and shades were drawn. Workmen could be seen entering and exiting the building at all times of the day and night. No one but old Ibram, the mosque's custodian, thought it strange that with so much activity, not very much debris came out.

World Teachings was known to operate in more than two dozen countries, raising funds and providing healthcare and education for impoverished children of the Muslim faith. Though Ibram wasn't all that familiar with the charity, he had heard of their good work. There was one additional function that neither Ibram nor the public knew about: World Teachings served as a front for the Sword of God.

No one outside of Jabal Hussein, not even Abud Rachman, knew of the existence of this particular cell. The people who went in and out of the building behind the mosque were responsible only to him. They were the most faithful of the faithful. If Rachman had suspected their purpose, he would have had all of them executed.

Ibram stopped his sweeping of the cobblestone walkway between the two buildings. He addressed the man in the white paint-splattered overalls standing outside the entrance, smoking a cigarette. He had often seen him and some of the other men taking a break, leaning against the building, in no hurry to get back to work.

No wonder the work was taking so long, he thought, *they spend most of their time smoking and talking.*

"How is the work coming?" Ibram asked, shifting his position to glance in through the door, which stood ajar. There was no progress since the last time he'd sneaked a look. Paint cans and drop cloths were still spread about much as they had been, but the interior was unchanged.

"Mind your own business, old man," the painter moved in front of him and closed the door.

There was something not right about these people, Ibram told himself.

"Get on with your sweeping," the man in the paint-splattered overalls said, taking a final drag on his cigarette. He dropped the burning cigarette on the ancient stones near his feet and ground it out with the toe of his boot, then went back inside, pulling the door shut behind him.

It was a slap in the face. Ibram was an old man, used to being ignored, but not like this. The painter had gone out of his way to insult him. *If I were twenty years younger,* Ibram thought. But he wasn't and he was certainly no match for the painter. There was nothing to do but continue on with his work. Reaching out, he swept the remnants of the discarded butt into the long-handled metal dustpan and cursed the man's ancestry. It was the best he could do.

A few moments later, working his way along the time-polished stones, still burning from the insult, he glanced up at the second-story window of the building. The cloth that covered the interior of the window had been pushed to one side. The face of the painter stared down at him.

CHAPTER TWENTY-FIVE

"YOU can't stay very long," the doctor instructed.

"I understand," Ari said.

"Mr. Barkan's still not very strong. By rights, I shouldn't be permitting —"

"Leave us," Jacob said from his hospital bed. The back of the bed was slightly raised and a pillow was propped up behind his head. His face looked bony from the weight he'd lost. He tried to sound assertive, but his voice was weak. The effort brought on a brief coughing spasm.

"You've only just reentered this world," the doctor countered. "Overextend yourself and you may well leave it again… permanently."

The coughing stopped, Jacob regained his composure. "I need to speak with him, alone. It's very important." Since he'd come out of the coma he'd been giving the doctors a hard time, demanding to see Ari.

"I must be out of my mind," the doctor ruminated.

"I won't be long," Ari promised.

"You've got five minutes," the doctor said, leaving them.

Ari pulled a chair alongside Jacob's bed. "You might try being a little nicer to the guy, he saved your life."

"I hear you're the one I have to thank for that. The nurse said you've been here nearly every day."

Ari was uncomfortable in the role of hero and savior. "How are you feeling?" he asked.

"Like a building fell on me."

"Part of one did," Ari said.

"My leg's pretty torn up."

"You won't be running any marathons," Ari said, "but then you never did. The doctor said that other than a slight limp, you'll be fine."

"The doctor gave us five minutes, we need to talk," Jacob said.

"It's more important you rest."

"I nearly had eternal rest —." The cough came back. Jacob waited for it to subside before continuing. "I'll rest later, right now you need to be quiet and listen to what I have to tell you." His agitation brought on another coughing spasm.

"All right, take it easy. What is it you want to tell me?"

"You can't leave Israel."

"I'm not going anyplace."

"Yes you are."

"You just work on getting well, we'll talk about it later," Ari said.

"By then it will be too late."

"Too late for what?"

"For you. Listen to me: I'm not who you think I am."

Jacob didn't sound like himself, but after what he'd been through Ari could certainly understand it. "You've been knocked about pretty badly —"

"I work for Israeli intelligence, a special branch of the Masad."

Ari couldn't help but laugh. "You're a teacher."

"My job was to watch you."

Ari played along. "For what reason?"

"Your work."

"My work at Ergoden is of interest to the Masad?"

"You don't work for Ergoden, you work for the government. You've been working on an alternative form of energy and you've had some sort of major breakthrough. I can't let you take that knowledge out of the country."

Jacob's delusional ranting suddenly stopped being amusing.

"How do you know all this?" Ari asked.

"Because it's what I do. It's my job to know."

Ari refused to believe him. "I told you at the restaurant that I'd made a breakthrough at work. You put two and two together —"

"You never told me it was in the field of energy or that you worked for the government. How did I know that?"

"I don't know."

"Why do you think I'm teaching in the same building you're doing your research in?" Ari didn't answer.

"Because your work makes you a security risk."

"You're telling me that all this time you've been spying on me?"

"You knew people would be checking up on you when you signed on."

"Not like this! You were supposed to be my friend!"

"I am your friend. If I weren't, you'd already be behind bars."

Things were spinning out of control; Ari tried to hold on.

"If you try to leave the country," Jacob said, "you'll be arrested and sent to prison. I won't be able to help you."

Ari struggled to make sense of what Jacob was telling him. *Who was this man?*

"You can't force me to stay in Israel," Ari said challengingly.

"You're wrong. You took an oath and you betrayed it." Jacob had no choice; he was determined to save Ari even if it meant destroying his world. "The girl's been using you to get her hands on your work."

"That's not true!"

"It is true," Jacob assured. "I'm sorry."

"You'd say anything to stop me, wouldn't you?"

"Yes, but that doesn't alter the fact: she's not to be trusted."

"What kind of person are you?" Ari exclaimed.

"One that loves his country and wants to save you. I have an obligation and so do you. She's selling you out."

"You know *nothing* about her."

"I know everything about her. Her name's Sidney Taylor, she works for RGI. The two of you have been having an affair for about a year." He had no other choice but to tell him everything. Ari had saved his life and he was going to repay him by ruining his.

"The whole time she's been with you, she's been having an affair with her boss. She's Roger Glass's mistress."

Ari got up, the chair toppled backwards. "Liar!"

For a moment, Jacob thought Ari was about to hit him. If he did there was nothing he could do to defend himself. Instead, Ari brought his hand down hard on the rail of the bed. The bed shook from the impact. Pain rocketed through Jacob's leg. He pushed through it.

"I should have let you bleed to death."

"Maybe, but it wouldn't change a thing: she's lied to you."

"Oh, and you didn't! I trusted you. You were supposed to be my friend!"

"I had no choice. She did!"

"We all have choices," Ari replied.

"She's after your discovery."

Ari backed away from the man he'd never really known. "You're wrong about her."

"If you don't believe me, ask her about her and Glass," Jacob said. He was struggling to breathe. The stress had been too much for him. "If after... if you still want more proof... I'll give it to —"

He couldn't finish, his body was racked by another fit of coughing.

"Are you okay?" Ari asked.

Jacob suddenly felt very tired. "I'll be fine," he managed to reply once his breath returned.

The door swung open and the doctor burst in.

"What the hell's going on in here? I told you he needed rest. His condition is delicate enough without you making matters worse."

"I was just going," Ari said, reaching down and picking up the chair that had fallen over. The doctor checked Jacob's vital signs.

"Leave me alone!" Jacob ordered, pushing away the doctor's hands.

"One more word out of you Mr. Barkan and I'll have you restrained." He turned to Ari.

"Please go."

"I am." Ari started for the door.

— 169 —

"You're leaving me no choice," Jacob called after him, pushing himself up from the bed. The effort was too much for Jacob. His body fell back towards the pillow. He found it impossible to keep his eyes open. He needed to rest, if only for a few moments.

"Nurse!" the doctor called.

It was the middle of the night in New York when Ari placed the call. *Had it all been a pack of lies? A bridge built of deceit about to fall?* He waited for Sidney's reply. The thought of the two of them being lovers burned at his gut.

"Well? Is it true?"

Ari sat on the edge of his bed in the room he now called home. The picture of David sat on the dresser, next to a half empty bottle of Scotch. He held the phone tightly to his ear, frightened of missing a word. His question continued to be met with silence.

Sidney struggled to support a world that was crashing down upon her. She had awakened from a dream to live a nightmare.

"You don't understand…"

"Yes or no? Are you two lovers?"

She sat in bed in the semidarkness of the room, hiding from the truth and Ari. "We were, but it's over."

"When were you going to tell me?"

Never, she thought, but said nothing.

"The whole time we were together, the whole time you were saying you loved me, it was only to get my discovery for *him*?"

"No! It's not like that. I love you. You have to believe me!"

But he didn't. Jacob had been right.

"I knew Roger before you and I met. I tried to break it off. I wanted to tell you, but I was frightened I'd lose you."

"Me or the fuel cell?"

"What I felt for you never had anything to do with that. I didn't even know about it until you told me."

"And the first thing you did was to run to him to tell him about my discovery. How the *hell* could you ask me to work for him!"

"He found out about us. He was furious and threatened to hurt you. I told him in order to protect you."

"To protect me!"

"It's true."

"What do you know about truth? It was always the money."

"No! I love you, I swear to God —" The tears ran down her cheeks. She wanted to pull the covers over her and hide from the world. She wanted to hide from Roger. Hide from Ari's accusations.

"I didn't want you to find out about Roger. I made a mistake. I should have told you. He promised to leave us alone if you brought your discovery to RGI —"

"I can't believe what a fool I've been! I've thrown away everything for you: my family, my career, even my country. I betrayed them all. For what?"

"Please listen," she begged.

The new fuel cell he'd discovered was to be his crowning moment. It had become his disgrace. He moved the phone away from his ear, distancing himself from the lure of her voice. She was going on, explaining what could never be explained. He placed the receiver back onto its cradle.

Ari sat, unable to move, descending deeper and deeper into an ocean of despair. Time and place no longer meant anything. The phone was ringing. He made no effort to answer it. Seven, eight, ten times it rang. Finally, it stopped.

CHAPTER TWENTY-SIX

Though it was still too early for most people to be in their offices, Sidney Taylor knew she'd find Roger there. The sun may well have set on the British Empire, but for RGI, it was still shining brightly.

She didn't wait to be announced. There was no one at the desk outside Roger's office to announce her. Dietricht Boch was sitting alone in the area of the room reserved for small, informal meetings. Papers were spread out on the table before him.

"Where is he?" Sidney said approaching Boch. She didn't care much for Dietricht and knew the feeling was mutual.

"Nature calls for king and commoner alike. You're in early," he remarked. In reality, he was surprised to see her at all. After what she'd done, he'd expected Roger to bar the door. For some reason unknown to Dietricht, he hadn't.

She commandeered one of the empty chairs and sat down. "I'll wait."

"We're in the middle of a meeting."

She didn't respond, merely crossed her legs and waited for Roger to return.

You'll get yours, Dietricht thought. It wasn't the time to get into a pissing match with her, there was far too much at stake for that. He ignored her presence and returned to organizing the pages on the table before him.

He'd leveraged himself to the hilt. Bet everything he could beg, steal and borrow on the upward play of oil in the futures market. When the Middle East exploded, he'd make a fortune. Nothing was more important than that. *Certainly not the bitch sitting across from him.*

The door to Roger's bathroom opened and he entered his office. He was surprised to see Sidney waiting for him. "Good morning, Sidney," he said, quickly recovering.

She got up from the chair. "Sorry to interrupt your meeting, Roger, but I need to speak with you in private."

"I'm afraid now's not a very good time," Roger said, approaching her.

"I tried to tell her," Dietricht chimed in.

"It's important," Sidney insisted.

"How about in an hour? We should be through —"

"I'll be gone by then."

"Where are you going?"

She glanced over at Dietricht, then back to Roger. "Two minutes is all I'm asking."

"If it's really that urgent —"

"It is," Sidney replied.

"Dietricht," Roger began. He didn't have to finish the sentence; Dietricht Boch had already started gathering together the papers on the table.

"Leave them where they are," Roger instructed. "I'll buzz you when we're through." He sat down and indicated for Sidney to do the same.

Dietricht looked across at Sidney. The bitch had won. As he got up to leave, their eyes met. She read the hostility in them. It was of no importance to her. She waited until the door closed before beginning.

"Ari knows."

"Knows what?"

"About us."

Roger leaned back against the chair. "How?"

"I don't know. At first, I thought you told him."

"Me? What would I have to gain by doing that?"

She'd asked herself the same question hours earlier and couldn't find a reasonable answer. "Nothing."

"What did he say?"

"He thinks we conspired to steal his discovery. He hung up on me."

"Call him back."

"I tried, he won't speak to me."

"What about the fuel cell?" Roger asked.

"You can forget about it."

"Has he told anyone else about it?"

It was an odd question, Sidney thought. "You're not hearing what I'm saying: he's not coming, and you're not getting his discovery. He wants nothing more to do with either of us."

It didn't matter, Roger told himself. *In a little while Ari Ben Lev and his fuel cell would simply cease to be a problem.*

"Aren't you going to say something?" Sidney demanded.

"What do you expect me to say? I can't force him to work for us."

It wasn't the response she'd expected. She thought he'd be all over her, threatening them both with God knows what.

"You surprise me, Roger. What about our deal? I can't deliver on it."

"Forget our deal. Come back to me and I'll forgive everything." It was a generous offer, but an impossibility for Sidney.

"I can't, Roger." She got up to go. "My plane leaves shortly for Israel."

"Israel?" Roger got to his feet. "You can't go to Israel!"

Again his reaction surprised her. "Given what's at stake," Sidney said, "I'd have frankly thought you'd be the first to encourage me to go."

Roger felt nothing for Ari or the faceless masses in Israel. The man had stolen from him, threatened to destroy a lifetime's work. *He deserved what he got but not Sidney.* In spite of everything, he loved her. He'd planned to comfort her, offer a shoulder to cry on when it was all over. Eventually, she'd have come back to him but not if she got on that plane.

"Wait a few days. Give him time to cool down."

"I've got to go," she said, turning to leave.

He grabbed her arm. "You can't!"

Sidney looked at him as if he'd lost his mind. He released his hold on her. *There was no other choice if he was to stop her.*

"We received word from one of our people of a possible terrorist attack in Jerusalem. If it comes it will be within the next few days."

The news had no impact on her resolve. "Terrorist attacks are hardly uncommon in that part of the world," she said.

"This one is different." The attack won't be conventional. Do you understand what I'm saying?"

Sidney shook her head.

"It could be nuclear," Roger clarified.

"You can't possibly be serious?"

"The man who brought us the information has always been reliable. I suggest you stay here until we know for certain."

"What about the Israelis?"

"I've had our people pass along the information," he lied. "It's in the hands of the Israeli government now."

"There's been nothing in the news?"

"There wouldn't be. Can you imagine the mass hysteria it would create if word of this got out? Even if it was a false alarm, hundreds would be killed and injured in the ensuing panic."

"What if your information's correct?"

"All the more reason for you not to go."

She hesitated, but only for a moment. "Ari's there. His child lives in Jerusalem. I've got to warn him."

"Don't be a fool!" He tried to hold on to her. "Didn't you hear anything I just told you?"

"What am I supposed to do, stay here with you and wait?"

"It makes more sense than getting on that plane. Let the Israelis do their work —"

"I can't."

"You'd risk everything to warn him?" Roger asked in disbelief.

"I love him," Sidney stated flatly.

He'd offered her life and she still chose Ben Lev over him. They could go to hell together! He let her go.

CHAPTER TWENTY-SEVEN

Ibram's room was located in the basement of the mosque. He'd come to think of it as home, although, in truth, there was little there of his own. The iron bed with its misshapen mattress, the bookshelf, the chair, even the small rug, belonged to the mosque. Only the framed pictures of his family, which were spread out across the top of his dresser, were his. The number of pictures had grown along with his children's respective families. He and his wife, whom Allah had called to heaven, had been blessed with four sons, two daughters and eighteen grandchildren. His children were dutiful and each had at one time asked him to live with them. He preferred not to burden them and enjoyed his independence. Perhaps he would reconsider their offers when he could no longer handle his duties at the mosque, but that was still years away. For the time being, he was content with the room that had been provided for him. Within those walls he had his pictures and his privacy.

The mosque was dark. He had locked up and turned off the lights hours ago, as he did every night before retiring to his room. Only this night, he hadn't been able to sleep.

Ibram made his way from his room up the dimly lit flight of stone stairs to the heavy wooden door at the rear of the mosque. The door opened onto the narrow pathway between the mosque and the building rented by World Teachings. He pushed open the door and stepped outside into the cool night air. Carefully he shut the door behind him, cutting off what little light escaped from within the mosque. Instantly, he became one with the black void between the buildings.

The air was cold against his skin. He regretted not having dressed warmer but it wasn't worth the effort to turn back now for his sweater.

Still, he worried about getting a cold. He couldn't afford to lose a day's pay.

Shaking off the chill in the air, he crossed the cobblestones and stopped before the door to the old building. The last of the workmen had left around suppertime. The building was shut down and locked. He remained standing before the door, listening. There wasn't a sound from within. The only thing he heard was the wind between the two buildings.

It was wrong of him to do what he was about to do. If the elders found out they would be extremely upset. Still, he needed to satisfy his curiosity. *There was something about these people....* He would take a quick peek, then he would leave. Surely there could be no harm in that. In and out, and no one would be the wiser.

The renters had re-keyed the cylinder but had left the old locking mechanism in place. It posed no problem for him. In no time, the door was open. He slipped quietly inside, pulling it shut behind him. The electricity was probably working but he didn't dare turn on the lights. He reached into his pocket, took out a packet of matches and lit one. The room came into view.

Absolutely nothing had been done. Tarps and paint cans stood about but the walls and ceiling were untouched. The lack of progress took him by surprise.

He took it all in until the match burned his fingers. Ibram shook it out and let it fall. He stepped back, knocking over a can. It was empty and offered no resistance. The can rolled along the floor, coming to a stop with his heart. His fear was amplified by the blackness surrounding him. He wanted to leave but didn't. The silence encouraged him. He lit another match and slowly ascended the flight of stairs to the floor above. Nothing had been done there either, the paint was peeled, the plaster still crumbling.

Ibram stood at the top of the landing. The second match went out. Not bothering to light a third, he carefully felt his way along the wall, down the hallway. His hand met the doorframe. He had come to the room from which the painter had stared down at him. He felt for the doorknob, found it, and slowly turned the handle. The door opened and Ibram entered. He lit another match.

This time, it was not the condition of the room that surprised him, but the strangeness of what he saw. A wooden crate, stamped with the letters of a language he did not know, stood against one wall. There were tables piled with tools and electronic equipment. On one of the tables rested a shiny metal cylinder from which a series of multicolor wires ran to a box. The place looked like the back room of an appliance repair shop.

The match burned out and Ibram immediately lit another. The scene that reappeared was still a mystery to him. He approached the table to get a better look and moved the match up and down the object that lay there. He reached out to touch it.

"Don't!" a voice behind him ordered. A light went on. Ibram dropped the match. He turned to face the workman from the other day. He hadn't heard him come up behind him. A second man stood by the door, his hand on the light switch. Ibram's first reaction was embarrassment.

"You couldn't leave it alone, old man, could you?" the painter said, driving the blade into Ibram's chest.

Ibram was aware of a searing pain. He felt his strength leaving him. He opened his mouth but a hand clamped firmly over it, preventing his scream. The blade was withdrawn and plunged in again.

"Are you insane?" the man by the door shouted at Kamaal. It was one of the half-dozen names the painter used.

Kamaal lowered the old man to the floor. He was dead by the time his head made contact.

"What would you have me do? He saw the bomb!"

"He couldn't possibly know what it is."

"I can't take that chance." Kamaal wiped the blood from the blade onto his paint-stained pants, and put the knife away. Then he bent down and began searching the old man's pockets. The man by the door moved closer, drawn like a moth to a flame.

"I agreed to do a *specific* job, I never agreed to this!"

"Silence," Kamaal commanded. The search of Ibram's pockets yielded nothing. "You build a bomb to kill tens of thousands and you whine about the death of one old man who's outlived his time."

"I'm a scientist, not an assassin," Zaeef said.

"You're a whore," Kamaal replied. 'You've been paid, now do as your're told!"

They had paid him $200,000 for a job that anyone with a graduate degree in nuclear engineering could do. Had he turned them down, others would have been only too happy to take their money.

Zaeef had worked for Pakistan's nuclear power authority until a second round of cutbacks had cost him his job. *It was their fault he was doing this,* he told himself. *What choice did he have? He had a family.* He'd assumed the bomb was nothing more than a bargaining chip to be played against Israel and its benefactor, the United States. No one would be crazy enough to actually use it. Only now, he was no longer so sure. If he could have given back the money and turned the clock back, he would have.

"Give me a hand," Kamaal said, taking the old man's legs. "We'll take him down to the basement."

Zaeef held back.

"Take his arms!" It was a command that left no room for being disobeyed.

Zaeef reluctantly bent down and took Ibram's arms. He lifted, and the old man's head fell back as his body rose from the floor. The old man's eyes, fixed eternally, stared up at him.

CHAPTER TWENTY-EIGHT

BEFORE boarding the plane, she had e-mailed a brief message telling Ari that she was on her way. *If you've ever loved me, please be there.* Frightened of saying the wrong thing, she kept it short, giving her flight number and arrival time. If he wasn't at the airport when her plane landed she'd go to where he was living. She had the name of the hotel. If he wasn't there, she'd camp out at his office until he agreed to listen.

Sidney Taylor sat in the darkened cabin draining her third Bloody Mary. She looked around. Most of the passengers were sleeping peacefully. *If only she was as lucky.* It was an impossibility. Every time she closed her eyes she had the most horrible nightmares. The thought of reentering the world of dreams was enough to keep her up.

Something else was bothering her as well. It was a question that had no logical answer and, as a scientist, logic was her religion. *Why hadn't Roger warned Ari? It should have been his first impulse.* Until she had told him otherwise, Roger hadn't the faintest idea that the deal with Ari was off. As far as he knew, Ari was still bringing him the keys to the kingdom. *So why hadn't he lifted a finger to get him out of there?* It didn't make sense.

The plane landed and Sidney Taylor was the first to clear customs. She stood in the hall and looked around. When she saw Ari she gave a prayer of thanks. He was drawn and haggard looking. There were dark circles under his eyes from an obvious lack of sleep and his clothes were wrinkled.

"I wasn't sure you'd come," she said as she approached him. It felt awkward not to kiss him hello, but he made no effort in that direction so neither did she.

"I almost didn't." He'd come to convince himself that he was through with her. Looking at her now, feeling his heart race at the sight of her, he wasn't as certain as he'd been on the ride to the airport.

"It's good to see you," Sidney said, hoping to hear a like reply. It didn't materialize.

"Your message said it was urgent."

"It is."

He was unwilling to be taken in a second time by her.

"Then I suggest you get on with it."

"Why were you so quick to judge me?" she asked. "I might not have been everything you thought I was but I'm certainly not the person you make me out to be. I don't deny I made mistakes but I never lied about loving you."

"I don't have time for this," Ari replied. Frightened of being drawn back in, he wanted to believe her.

"Can you really tell me you feel *nothing* for me?" Sidney asked.

"No, I feel something. Contempt."

He wounded himself with the pain he inflicted. He was being horrid and he knew it, but it was his only defense against her. And yet, looking at her, it was hard to maintain the pretense. She seemed so vulnerable, so lovely. How easily he crossed back and forth over that thin line that separated love from hate. But in spite of how much his body wanted her, it was impossible to see her standing in front of him without also wanting to strangle her.

"Why did you come?" he asked.

"Because of you... because of us."

"If those are your only reasons for coming, I could have saved you the trip."

She struggled to keep what little control of her emotions she had left. She didn't want to break down and cry.

"You wouldn't take my calls?"

"That should have told you something."

"This isn't like you," Sidney said.

"I've become the person you've made me," Ari replied. "If this is all you wanted to discuss —"

"It's not. There's something far more important than us." She looked around, people were constantly moving by them. "Is there someplace private we can talk?"

It was impossible for him to continue on as he had, being the instrument of her pain. "There's a small waiting area not far from here, we can talk there."

"Can't we go to your hotel?"

"That's not going to happen." He didn't trust her, but he trusted himself even less.

"I'm not thinking about that," Sidney said. "I just thought it would be someplace quiet where we —"

"A quiet corner is the best I can offer."

There wasn't time to waste arguing; she followed him.

"And you really expect me to believe all of this?" Ari leaned forward in his chair, closing the distance between them. Sidney sat in the seat opposite him. They spoke in guarded whispers.

"You think I'm making it up!"

"The possibility crossed my mind."

"Why would I invent such a story?"

"You tell me."

"If you don't believe me, make some calls. You must know people in your government who can confirm what I've told you."

Jacob Barkan came to mind. He'd vowed never speak to him again but there was too much at stake to let personal feelings get in the way. "There is one person I can ask," Ari said.

"Then do it, but do it fast. I don't know much time is left for you and your family to get out of Jerusalem."

In spite of himself, he was beginning to believe her. "If what you're saying is true, why hasn't there been any announcement? There's been nothing in the media."

"I've already told you, your government doesn't want a panic on its hands."

"It doesn't make sense."

"Why? Because you can't accept that I'm trying to help you?"

Ari leaned closer until their faces were only inches apart. "Probably, and because where you're concerned, I've learned to look for the price tag."

Sidney struck out, instinctively. Ari grabbed her wrist, stopping her. "That's the first emotion of yours I can really trust." He released her.

She was losing it. "Why are you being like this?"

She had ruined his life and she was asking him why he was behaving badly?

"How do you expect me to behave? I trusted you, and because of that I've lost my family, I'm about to lose my job, and I'm one step away from being thrown into prison for sedition. And now you come to me with this story —"

"Roger didn't volunteer that information, he told me because he didn't want me getting on that plane." She couldn't hold it together any longer. She began to cry.

If it was an act, it was a convincing one. "I'm sorry, but it just doesn't make any sense," Ari said.

"Why?" She wiped at her tears.

"What would the reaction of your government be if they got warning that a nuclear attack might be directed against Washington?"

"They'd take the threat more seriously than you seem to."

"You bet they would. On September 11 they moved your president and vice president out of Washington, didn't they?"

"So?"

"There's been no such action taken here. The Knesset is still in session and the prime minister is in attendance. Does that sound like they received any warning?"

"No, but —"

"But what?" Ari asked. Sidney couldn't argue with his logic. She was back to the question that had troubled her from the beginning. *Why hadn't he warned Ari?* And then everything fell into place for her.

"Oh my God!"

"What is it?"

All the blood had left Sidney's face. "Roger never informed your government. He wants it to happen."

"Why would he want such a thing?"

"Because Roger's whole life is oil, and you've threatened it. Without you and your fuel cell —" She didn't bother to finish. Sidney got to her feet.

"You've got to believe me, there's going to be an attack on Jerusalem and your government has no idea!"

He did believe her. There was no time to waste; he got up. He would take her to see Jacob.

"Ari Ben Lev?"

A man he'd never seen before approched him. A second man stood off to one side. The two were obviously together. There was an officiousness about them, the straightness of their backs, the similar dress.

The man flipped open a credit card sized case and offered Ari his credentials. The government ID looked official, though Ari wouldn't have known a forgery from the real thing.

"I need for you and Ms. Taylor to accompany me," the man said.

"How do you know my name?" Sidney asked, moving closer to Ari.

"If you'll come with us quietly, everything will be explained," the second man said, taking Sidney's arm.

"Get your hands off of her," Ari demanded, pulling Sidney to him. "Neither of us is going anywhere with you until you tell us what this is all about."

"I'm afraid that's not an option," the man before Ari replied. "Now if you plea —"

"Come on." Ari took Sidney's hand, pulling her with him, attempting to get by the man blocking his way.

"You leave me no choice. You and Ms. Taylor are under arrest." The man took hold of Ari's arm. His grip was like a vice. His partner reached for Sidney, pulling her away from Ari.

"Arrest for what?" Ari demanded.

"For the theft of Israeli national secrets."

"Did Jacob send you?" Ari asked.

"Just come with us," the man replied, moving Ari along. Sidney was being pulled in another direction.

"Ari!" Sidney called.

"Leave her alone!"

People were staring. Ari began to struggle. "I need to speak with Jacob Barkan! There's a bomb —" The words barely escaped his lips before he found himself on the floor.

Guns were drawn. Pandemonium spread. The mention of a bomb and a man being thrown to the ground was all it took. People began running, trying to escape the area.

Ari noticed none of it. He lay face down on the floor, aware of a sharp pain. His arms were being handcuffed behind him. He struggled to no avail. Strong hands lifted him to his feet. He could hear Sidney calling out to him, but he was being pulled along, unable to see her. There was nothing he could do as he was pushed and dragged through the terminal to the waiting van.

CHAPTER TWENTY-NINE

Ari sat on the bed in his cell, his face buried in his hands. He was defeated by the reality of his helplessness. Those who'd kept him isolated, ignoring his shouts, had squandered precious hours. No one had answered his pleas. He'd railed until his voice gave out. Was there anyone beyond the bolted doors who even heard? If they did, it didn't seem to matter to them that they all were going to die.

He hadn't been able to get word out to Hannah to take David and leave the city. They were doomed with the rest, and in the end, it was he who had doomed them. He wasn't religious but he began to pray. He prayed for the innocents on both sides and for Israel. He thought of Sidney. He loved her. In a little while none of it would matter.

For his entire life, all he'd wanted was to make a difference: to leave some part of himself behind so that when he was gone his life would be more than a vanishing ripple on the surface of the water. His teachers, his parents, Hannah, all of them had continued to believe in him long after he'd stopped believing in himself. And then to finally succeed after all those years of struggle. His fuel cell had offered the prospect of redemption. Instead, he would leave behind unbelievable suffering. His legacy would be the slaughter of millions of innocents.

Racked by anguish and regret he got off the bed. He stood motionless for a moment then walked to wall. He pressed the palms of his hands against the roughly hewn stone, his fingers spreading out flat, as if the stones would fall away before him and a door to heaven would suddenly open. Ari bowed his head and rested it against the wall. The coolness of the stone offered some relief from the burning in his head. He was a reflection of the endless line of Jews who for centuries had come to pray at the Western Wall of the Old Temple.

His mind carried him through the streets and buildings of Jerusalem, the golden city that for millennia people had fought and died for. It was like looking directly into the sun, nothing would be left. He'd dedicated his life to science. Discovered a new source of energy. It was a gift meant to change the world, not to end it.

He lifted his head and brought it back down hard against the rough-hewn stones. Again, and again, he brought it to bear, punishing himself until the skin of his forehead split and the stones were streaked with his blood.

The cell door banged open and the guards rushed in. Ari took no notice; his praying continued.

*   *   *

Sidney, too, struggled with her confinement. She had all but given up trying to reach her captors when the door to her cell opened and a uniformed soldier entered. Her first thought was that he had come to execute her.

"Please come with me," the guard instructed, holding the door open.

Sidney held back. She'd been demanding to be released the whole time she'd been locked up like an animal in a cage . Now, when she'd been ordered to leave her cell she was too frightened to go. *This was Israel, not some feudal Arab monarchy.* But it was still the Middle East, the place where children strapped explosives around their waist and walked into family restaurants.

"Where are you taking me?" she demanded.

"No one is going to harm you," he said, sensing her fear. The words were meant to reassure her, but they didn't. Reluctantly, she exited her cell and stepped into the hallway. The guard reached behind her and shut the door with finality. It echoed like the report of a gun. She walked alongside him, down the dimly lit hallway, past other cells she imagined were identical to hers.

"My government is going to hear about this," Sidney threatened. He didn't break stride or bother to answer. Her warning had failed to impress him. They reached a flight of stairs. Sidney's legs, weak with fear, could barely climb them. He took her arm to help her.

"What have you done with my things?" Sidney asked.

"Your belongings are waiting for you," he said as they ascended the stairs.

"Where?"

"Everything will be explained shortly."

The steps led to another hallway and a metal door at the far end.

"I'm not going any farther," Sidney said. "Not until you tell me where you're taking me!"

Things like this didn't happen in her world. People didn't arrest you and lock you away for no reason. They didn't deprive you of your rights or keep you from speaking with a lawyer. *These people could make her disappear and nobody would ever know!*

"You're almost there, Ms. Taylor," the soldier said. He unlocked the heavy door and held it open for her. Light streamed in from the alleyway behind the building.

"Please, Ms. Taylor, no one's going to harm you."

She looked into his eyes and saw his discomfort. *If they were going to kill her, why didn't they just do it quickly.* She approached the door and stepped across the threshold into the daylight. She could see the waiting car and the two men standing alongside it. The driver stood by the opened rear door, waiting for her. The second man, his back towards her, was speaking on a cell phone. He ended his conversation, put the phone away and turned in her direction. A hideous scar ran down his face.

She had no intention of going with these people. She turned, but it was too late, the door through which she'd entered had closed and the man who had brought her here had disappeared behind it. She was alone and there was no place to go but forward.

"Please get in the car," the man with the scar said.

She didn't move. "I demand to speak with someone in authority."

"That would be me," Lazarus replied.

"Who are you?"

"You can call me Lazarus." He spoke softly, unthreateningly, cognizant of the frightened bird within his grasp.

"I work for the Israeli government." He motioned to the open car door. "We can talk on the way."

Sidney hesitated. She glanced back at the locked door behind her.

"I'm not going to hurt you," he assured.

"I wish you people would stop saying that, it makes it a little difficult to believe."

He smiled. "Nevertheless, it's true."

Despite the horrible scar, there was something disarming in his smile. She approached the car, hesitated momentarily, then climbed into the back seat of the vehicle.

Lazarus got in beside her. The other man closed the door. Sidney watched him come around to the driver's side and get in behind the wheel.

"Where are you taking me?"

"All in good time," Lazarus replied.

"Don't you people ever answer a question directly?"

Again, Lazarus smiled. It made the scar more pronounced. He saw her looking at it.

"An old gift. Arab hospitality," he explained.

Sidney looked away, embarrassed. "I'm sorry. I didn't mean to stare."

"I'm used to it," Lazarus said. He leaned forward, towards the driver and said something to him in Hebrew. The car pulled out of the alleyway and entered the stream of traffic.

Lazarus kept watch on the changing buildings and the people in the street. He was a cautious man who took his job extremely seriously. His phone rang. He answered, never taking his eyes from the changing world outside the car.

The ensuing conversation was heated. Something had obviously happened that didn't please him, but since he spoke in Hebrew, Sidney had no idea of what it was.

The car exited the city and sped up. Lazarus put the phone away.

"You've caused my government a lot of trouble Ms. Taylor."

"I don't know how. I came here to warn —"

"You came here to convince one of our scientists to turn over secrets to you on a project he's been working on."

"That's not true!"

"You wanted him to leave Israel. To go to America and work for the company you work for."

Did everyone know everything about her life?

"There's no crime in that," Sidney replied.

"Ari Ben Lev's discovery belongs to Israel."

"It belongs to him. He developed it and he should be the one who decides what to do with it."

"That's charmingly naive of you, Ms. Taylor. However, Ari Ben Lev signed and then violated the terms of an agreement that can send him away for the next twenty years, if my government chooses to exercise that option."

"Is that your intention, to make him a prisoner?"

"If I were you, Ms. Taylor, I'd be worrying right now about your own future."

"I'm an American citizen."

"I'll do whatever it takes to protect my country," Lazarus answered calmly.

"Including kidnapping an American?"

"Yes, including that."

She wondered if it also included making people disappear permanently.

"What do you intend to do with me?" she asked.

"That depends entirely on you."

"We've done nothing wrong," she insisted. "We just wanted to be together."

Lazarus was losing his patience. "It can still be arranged. You can share his cell."

"You can't —"

"I can, and I will if I have to. My country's at war. Undeclared, but a war just the same. You don't come here, try to harm it, and then wave your American passport in my face."

"I'm not trying to harm anyone. To the contrary, I came here to help."

"You seem to have done a *wonderful* job of that, haven't you?"

Sidney didn't reply.

"There are things at stake right now that are far more important than you and your love life, Ms. Taylor."

"I realize that. It's what I've been trying to tell you people for hours. Jerusalem is going to be attacked!"

"We've heard you."

"I didn't think anyone was listening."

"We've been listening."

"So what are you people doing about it?"

"The information has been relayed to the proper authorities, but that's not my immediate concern right now."

"*Relayed?* Are you out of your mind? I'm telling you, people are going to attack your country with a nu —"

"What people?" Lazarus asked. "Islamic Jihad? Hamas? Who?"

"I don't know who."

"Then maybe you can tell me when the attack is coming, or how the bomb is to be delivered. Missile? Plane? Federal Express?"

"You think this is a joke?" Sidney shot back.

"No, Ms. Taylor, it's no joke."

He already had the answers to the questions he'd asked her. He could have told her as much but his job wasn't to give information. She offered him nothing but an additional headache, which he longed to be rid of.

"Then what are you doing to stop it?"

"We are attending to the matter."

He had a way of saying things with a matter-of-factness that simply infuriated her. She was angry. Angry that no one had listened to her. Angry at being the pawn of men like Roger and this man who called himself Lazarus.

"We're almost here," the driver interrupted.

They had turned onto the approach road to Ben-Gurion International Airport. Sidney looked out the window and then questioningly at Lazarus.

"You're going back to America, Ms. Taylor," he said.

She was flooded with an instantaneous sense of relief. "I don't understand. You're just letting me go? Why?

"Because you are one of those well-intentioned people, Ms. Taylor, who cause problems for everyone who gets close to them. You're like a rose that invites with its fragrance and sticks with its thorn. In short, you're trouble, Ms. Taylor, and that's one thing Israel doesn't need more of."

How dare he! No one had ever spoken to her like that. And yet she'd be hard pressed to deny his accusation. This man with the monstrous scar, who barely knew her, knew her better than most. She loved Ari and had practically destroyed him.

"Please don't come back," Lazarus said. "If you do, if you ever set foot on Israeli soil again, I promise you I'll see to it that you spend the rest of your days in a cell like the one you just left."

"What about Ari?"

"He's no longer a concern of yours. I suggest you forget about him."

"I won't."

"If you really love him, you'll get on the plane and cause him no more trouble."

She was in no position to argue. For the time being, at least, she would do as he asked. When she got safely back to the United States she would contact a lawyer, or the Justice Department, or anyone who would listen to her.

The car pulled in front of the terminal and came to a stop. A man waiting for them immediately approached the vehicle. He looked in, making eye contact with Lazarus.

"Would you please come with me, Ms. Taylor," the man said opening the door for her. His job was to make certain she made her flight.

They were all so polite, she thought. Killers with manners. She got out of the car.

"Have a good trip, Ms. Taylor," Lazarus offered, his face framed in the open rear window. She glanced silently back at him and the scar that was such a prominent part of his features.

"Don't write and don't come back," he warned a final time as his driver pulled away from the curb.

CHAPTER THIRTY

JABAL experienced the familiar surge of excitement he associated with going into battle: part anticipation, part danger. It heightened all his senses and made him more keenly aware of things around him. The sensation was primal. He exalted in it as an addict exalts in his drug.

"It's time," Jabal said, checking his sidearm. He ran the gun through a quick weapons check that had become second nature to him.

Iradj Bin Rab stood by the blanket-covered window, across the spartan room from Jabal. Moving aside the material that blacked out the world outside, he looked out onto the street. Nothing was moving. The street was empty of life. Man and animal had been driven by the relentless heat to seek whatever shade could be found.

Unlike Jabal, it was not excitement that Iradj was feeling. He was frightened, and for good reason: It was too late to turn back. He wished to God it was over.

"You're certain the bomb's functional," he asked, releasing the makeshift curtain and letting it fall back into place. The street disappeared. He turned towards Jabal.

"It's functional." Jabal repositioned the gun's magazine, heard it click into place and then chambered a bullet.

Iradj wiped the sweat from his face. It wasn't just the heat that was getting to him. "And our people in Jerusalem?"

"They are ready."

"Can we be certain?"

"Only death is certain," Jabal replied with annoyance, holstering the revolver and wondering if Iradj could be counted on to do what was required of him.

"Are you having second thoughts?" Jabal said, approaching Iradj.

Iradj averted his eyes. "Of course not." It would have been a mistake for him to say anything else.

"I'm relieved to hear that," Jabal said.

"It's only that perhaps we should wait a bit longer." He noted the look on Jabal's face. "I mean, until the actual detonation. There will be confusion, chaos. It will make what we have to do easier."

"It will make it harder," Jabal corrected. "Abud will instantly close ranks. The time to act is now. We will have only one chance," Jabal reminded him. "A few seconds either way will be the difference between success or failure, living or dying."

"I understand."

"I hope you do." Jabal sniffed the air. "Because you stink of fear."

"Any sane person would be frightened. Abud is not one to take lightly."

"Neither am I," Jabal replied. He poked two fingers against Iradj's chest, over his heart. "Abud will not be your problem if you fail me."

Iradj stepped back, away from Jabal. "I won't."

"For both our sakes, I hope you are right."

"It's time," Jabal said, heading for the door.

It exploded inward. Armed soldiers pushed their way through. Jabal had little time to react. Before his hand could reach his gun, the butt of a rifle connected with his face, breaking his nose and sending him sprawling. Soldiers were instantly upon him, lifting him to his feet and disarming him. Others trained automatic rifles on Iradj, who made no effort to resist. It would have been useless and certain death to do otherwise. Iradj raised his hands, offering no excuse for anyone to misinterpret his intentions.

Jabal fought through the pain. He attempted to wipe away the blood that flowed down his face from his broken nose. He got a rifle butt in the chest for his effort.

"Keep your hands up," the soldier shouted, his finger tightening on the trigger of his rifle.

"Easy," Jabal appealed, straightening up from the blow. "You've got the gun." He struggled to clear his head and regain his strength.

The soldier took a step back, keeping his gun pointed at Jabal. Two other soldiers, their guns ready, did the same. Jabal recognized them all.

"Abir," Jabal said, addressing one of the soldiers, "you are making a big mistake. I order you to put down your weapon!"

Abud Rachman entered the room. "The mistake is yours," he answered. "You're under arrest."

"For what?"

"For treason."

"Treason? There is no one more loyal to our cause than me. Let my accuser say his lies to my face."

"I accuse you," Abud Rachman said.

Jabal's face flushed with anger. He spit out the blood that had collected in his mouth. "It is not me who has betrayed our people."

"It's over," Rachman said. "I know about Jerusalem and I know about the bomb." What he saw in Jabal's eyes was pure hatred.

"Good!" Jabal said, not taking his eyes off Rachman. "I have no wish to deny our hour of greatness."

"Why have you done this?" Rachman asked.

"Because you lacked the courage to do it."

"It's not courage to do this thing, it's madness."

"You call it madness to destroy our enemies?" Jabal lowered his hands slightly. "If that's madness then I embrace it willingly. There was a time when you shared that madness."

"Never! You would destroy our homeland, the very thing we fight for?"

"And you would surrender it to the enemy. I call that traitorous."

"How could you destroy Jerusalem and our holy sights?"

"What is more holy than to rid our land of Jews? We will rebuild."

"And what do you think will happen when the bomb goes off?"

Abud asked.

"It will signal a new beginning!"

"It will signal an end," Rachman replied. "The Israelis will reply in kind."

"Against whom? They'll have no idea who is responsible."

"You are a fool! They'll do what you would in their place, target us all!"

"America wouldn't let them."

"America won't be able to stop them. No one will."

"Better to die a martyr than to live a frightened old man."

"You would condemn us all?"

Jabal addressed the soldiers guarding him. "You have heard!" He pointed at Rachman. "There stands your traitor. He who strikes him down will be rewarded both here and in heaven."

No one moved. Despite doubts that some of them may have had they were still loyal to Rachman.

"Fools!" He turned back to Rachman. "It doesn't matter. You're too late to stop what is to come. With or without your blessing the firestorm approaches."

"We have the location of the bomb," Rachman confided.

"You lie!"

"You know me better than that."

A cloud passed quickly across Jabal's face, then the sun appeared. "It doesn't matter. There isn't time enough for your people to cross into Israel to stop this." He'd won, even if he didn't live to see it.

"*Our people* won't have to. The Israelis have been informed, they will handle it."

"You warned our enemies?"

"You left me no choice."

Jabal tried to push past the soldiers guarding him, intent on killing Rachman with his bare hands. A rifle butt drove him to the ground before he could reach his target. He tried to rise, but the blows rained down.

"Enough!" Rachman ordered. The soldiers backed off.

Jabal lay crumpled like a piece of twisted rope on the floor. He struggled in vain to lift himself. Blood spattered his uniform and ran from a gash in his scalp. He was bloodied but still not defeated.

"Betrayer of Islam," he accused, barely able to get the words out.

"Allah alone will decide which of us has betrayed Islam," Rachman replied.

Jabal fought unsuccessfully to get up. He looked like a fish out of water. A soldier guarding him laughed.

"Stop it!" Iradj Bin Rab demanded, going to Jabal's aid. Rachman motioned his men not to stop him.

"He's a soldier," Iradj said, kneeling down and sliding his hand under Jabal's arm in an attempt to help his to his feet. *His death didn't need to be preceded by humiliation.*

"Who betrayed me?" Jabal asked Rachman.

Rachman's eyes moved involuntarily to Bin Rab. It was only for a moment, but a moment was all Jabal needed to see the truth.

"You?"

Iradj didn't answer.

No one saw the knife in Jabal's boot, or his hand pass over it. He whispered something to Iradj, the words barely audible.

"Allahu Akbar. *God is great!*" Jabal repeated, looking into the traitor's eyes. With what remained of his strength he drove the knife upward. The blade sliced through Iradj's shirt in search of his heart.

A single shot echoed in the small room. Rachman stood with the gun in his outstretched hand. There would be no trial for either man.

The front door of the building rented by World Teachings opened and a man came out to speak with one already standing outside. The scene was natural enough, two workmen taking a break. Neither man appeared to be in any great hurry.

Further down the narrow street, an old man, no longer able to straighten his back, made his way towards the mosque with the aid of his daughter. She bore his weight as her duty. Her face and body was respectfully covered in the Arab tradition. They were heading for afternoon prayers.

The workmen glanced momentarily at the pair but took no great interest in them. A mangy yellow mutt sniffed its way along the stones and stopped not far off. Ribs stuck noticeably out of an emaciated frame. The dog lifted its leg and began to take a piss against the wall.

"Get out of here!" the workman closest to the mutt shouted, stamping his foot. His friend bent down to pick up a stone.

The dog, interrupted in finishing his business, continued on. It kept an eye on the two men, taking a wide detour around them. The man with the stone threw it, hitting his mark. The dog yelped and moved quickly off. The men laughed.

Above them, the sun baked down and the air smelled of fresh tar from the roof of the building next door. It was being repaired. Men had been working on the roof all morning. One spread the hot tar with a long-handled broom while another rolled out the paper and a third man assisted. The noise and the smell had been annoying at first but had since blended into the day's routine.

Inside the building, on the ground floor, a couple of men sat on overturned empty paint buckets, finishing their tea. Their weapons rested beside them. A third man was in an adjoining room heating water on a kerosene burner for the changing shift.

One floor above, a man rested on a cot set up in the back room. His eyes were closed, his AK-47 leaned against the wall by his head. He rolled over on his side and continued to catch a few extra minutes of sleep. Down the hall in the room that held the bomb, Zaeef finished explaining the intricacies of the device's timing mechanism to Kamaal. Since the incident with the old man, Kamaal hadn't let him out of his sight. The Pakistani was no longer to be trusted. Given an opportunity, Kamaal was certain he'd run.

* * *

The exercise was conducted precision-like. No one could afford it be handled otherwise. The muffled shots came from a slightly opened window across the way. Only a small puff of white smoke gave away the location. The two terrorists who stood outside the building were the first to be eliminated. No attempt was made to take them alive. A small hole suddenly appeared in the center of one man's forehead, blood sprayed the wall behind where he stood. The second man barely had time to react, and no time to warn those inside. The bullet tore away half his throat and silenced him forever.

The old man passing by the building with his daughter suddenly straightened and was no longer old. An Uzi appeared from beneath his robes. The woman with him threw off her covering and was clothed in the uniform of an Israeli army officer. The workmen on the roof of the accompanying building had transformed into soldiers, exchanging their tools for weapons.

The best of Israel's elite antiterrorist task force, commandos trained in urban warfare, entered the building. Stun grenades preceded their attack. They moved quickly. Efficiently. Everyone was aware of the price of failure.

Part of the roof was blown in, raining shards of wood and plaster down on the man sleeping below. He rolled off the cot and grabbed his gun. Through the smoke, he could see soldiers descending on ropes from the gaping hole in the roof. The man fired at the dangling shadows. One fell like a rag doll. The remaining Israelis returned fire, raking the room. Bullets chewed up anything that moved. The noise was intense, the battle over almost before it began. There was no further resistance. Bursts of gunfire rang out from the floor below.

Jabal's men abandoned their tea for their weapons. One man was taken out before he reached his gun. The second was more successful. He fired, getting off a burst in the direction of the woman. His aim was faulty, hers wasn't. Bullets, like the fast-moving needle of a sewing machine, stitched a path across his chest, nearly cutting him in two.

Automatic fire caused the Isaelis to take cover. From the makeshift kitchen the remaining terrorist ran for the staircase and the safety of the higher floor. He continued to fire behind him as he hurriedly ascended the steps. He was halfway up before realizing what was waiting for him at the top. The flash of fire blew him backwards, sending him tumbling down the stairs. It had taken less than two minutes to secure the ground floor.

Upstairs, the door to the front room that housed the bomb was breached. It splintered and blew in. A young Israeli soldier, little more than a boy, was the first in. He was trained what to look for and what not to shoot at. Kamaal stood by the table, his arm around the Pakistani's neck, using him as a shield.

"Don't shoot!" Zaeef screamed. He was only a scientist; he didn't want to die.

The Israeli hesitated, Kamaal didn't. He didn't fire at the broader target that would be protected by a vest, but aimed higher. The bullet struck the Israeli in his neck and he went down.

Those behind him were not so reluctant to shoot. Bullets tore into Zaeef. His dream of two hundred thousand American dollars died with him. The high-velocity ordnance passed through him and into Kamaal.

Kamaal, unable to support the dead weight, abandoned his shield. He raised his gun.

The Israelis fired, granting him his wish for martyrdom.

"Situation stabilized, man down!" one of the soldiers shouted into his mouthpiece. The woman from downstairs, the officer in charge of the operation, pushed past her people and entered the room. She approached the fallen terrorist, her gun trained on him. She kicked away his weapon then prodded him with her boot. There was no movement. Placing her gun to his head, she bent down and put her fingers against Kamaal's neck. This one would give them no more trouble. It was over.

She got up and approached the table that held the device. She knew what it was, though she'd never seen one before. Her eyes followed the wires. The diodes of the device to which they led flashed red. The numbers were descending: twenty, nineteen, eighteen.

"Shit! It's alive," she said into her headset, backing away from the device as if it were a snake preparing to strike.

For one moment, everything stood still. Then it began. The oxygen ignited. Time expanded. The city trembled as if aware of its doom, then disappeared into a cloud of dust and heat. Stones that had stood for thousands of years melted. The Church of the Holy Sepulcher, the Dome of the Rock, the Western Wall, a remnant of the great Temple built by Herod, were all gone in an instant. Buildings rose, as if from the dead, and then disappeared forever. The sand upon which Jesus trod was turned into glass. A half million people, Christian, Arab and Jew alike, ceased to exist, vaporized into nothingness.

CHAPTER THIRTY-ONE

S IDNEY TAYLOR learned of the news 32,000 feet up. There was crackling of the plane's speaker system and then the captain got on to make the announcement. His voice was shaking. He could hardly get the words out. He'd been trained to project an image of control but it was an impossibility: His wife and the child she was carrying lived in Jerusalem. Silence followed the announcement. People throughout the cabin began to cry. The cries turned into wails for the dead.

The television monitor flashed news of the events in the Middle East. The satellite photos and the pictures they portrayed were horrific. Roger Glass sat in his office watching the screen. Dietricht Boch sat a little way off. Both men, like people all over the world, were riveted to the news, watching the breaking stories unfold.

"Devastation, beyond anything imaginable. The death toll will unquestionably reach into the hundreds of thousands. We are witnessing a human catastrophe of monumental proportions," the reporter announced. "We are still unclear as to what exactly has taken place. The only thing we know for certain at this point is that there has been some sort of nuclear explosion in Israel. The city of Jerusalem no longer exists."

"What's the current spot price?" Roger asked Dietricht.

"It's already spiked to over eighty dollars a barrel." Billions had just been added to the firm's bottom line, nineteen million to Dietricht's personal holdings.

"Israel's Knesset, the building that housed its parliament, is gone. How many in Israel's government are also gone is anyone's guess. It is known that most of the legislative body was in Jerusalem at the time of the blast. There are rumors that the Prime Minister and members of his cabinet had left the city prior to the explosion, but to date it remains only a rumor. If they didn't make it out, the big question is: Who's running the government?

"Unconfirmed sources say control has been handed over to the military until civilian control can be reestablished. We are unable to verify the accuracy of this information at this time." News was breaking fast. The announcer struggled to keep up.

"A high-placed source in the Kingdom of Saudi Arabia blames this disaster squarely on the Jewish State, claiming the bomb was quote, *an Israeli weapons experiment gone terribly wrong*. At the moment, there is no shortage of accusations and hearsay circulating, but it is difficult to know which, if any, of these stories are true.

"The situation in the Middle East is extremely volatile and changing rapidly. One moment, please." The reporter adjusted his earpiece. He sat perfectly still for a moment, listening.

"I've just been informed elements of the Syrian army have been mobilized and are moving towards Israel's northern boarder! Activity has also been reported to the south as Egyptian forces, too, seem to be mobilizing. Whether these moves are defensive or in preparation of something else is yet to be determined. Hezbollah, the armed Islamic organization openly financed and supported by Iran's religious leaders, has called for all Arabs to unite in jihad." The timber of the reporter's voice was rising. It was not a broadcasting technique.

"President Benton is asking for restraint and calm on both sides. Pressure is most assuredly being applied to Israel to refrain from lashing out before ultimate responsibility has been conclusively established."

He looked at the memorandum just placed before him. His comments became visceral. "My God! Word just in: Satellite reports have confirmed that the nuclear silos which Israel has to date denied it had, have just gone hot."

EPILOGUE

In life, things rarely work out as they're made to in stories. Happy endings are never certain: The good aren't always victorious, nor are the bad always vanquished. Planes commandeered by terrorists, flying towards towers of concrete and steel, don't veer off at the very last minute.

For Ari Ben Lev and his family there was no happy ending, nor for the millions of others drawn into the maelstrom. The world as we knew it had changed forever on that day. The oil fields of Iraq and Libya disappeared in a fireball, so did the cities of Teheran and Damascus. The dream of a Palestinian homeland vanished, along with over a million Palestinians. But for Roger Glass and Alexander Primikov, the newly elected president of Russia, oil was still king.